Until My Dying Day

S.C. Stokes

Prescient Publishing

CONTENTS

CHAPTER 1

Kasey ran down the street, the chaos of New York City under siege drowning out each lengthy stride.

The mayor had issued the evacuation order, but it was already too late.

Emptying the bustling metropolis in a matter of hours was proving an impossible task. City traffic had come to a complete halt as the bottlenecked bridges cut Manhattan off from the mainland.

Drivers abandoned their cars and fled on foot. Tempers flared as an impatient mob began to form. Trapped in the city, fights began to break out, while others smashed windows in an attempt to vent their anger.

Pedestrians screamed as they sought safety amid the devastated city, but there was none to be found. The entire city shook beneath her feet as the buildings looming above her teetered and swayed. The movement was unsettlingly in the extreme.

Beneath her feet, the ground shook as great chasms yawned open along the street. Burst pipes leaked into the street as the seismic activity grew in intensity.

Nearby, a manhole cover exploded upward like a cork finally freed from its champagne bottle. The heavy iron cover flipped through the air until it smashed into the hood of a parked taxi. From the broken cityscape, plumes of oily emerald smoke began to rise.

It's happening. I am too late.

Despite the freezing December air, beads of sweat ran down Kasey's brow. She had to keep running. So many lives depended on it. With his place on the Arcane Council taken from him and his identity unmasked, Akihiro had brought his plot to its devastating conclusion. Now, New York would pay the ultimate price.

The screech of tearing steel resounded from nearby. She slowed her pace and scanned her gaze in the direction of the noise.

The facade of the building beside her split open from the seismic upheaval. Windows shattered, raining glass down from above. Kasey shielded her face, but a large shard sliced into her left arm, drawing blood. She winced but there was little to be done now. As the building's structural integrity deteriorated, she picked up her pace. It would only be moments before the entire tower came crashing down.

Kasey tore her eyes from the building and focused on the street ahead.

A piercing wail split the evening air. It was far too shrill for an adult. When it came again, the scream cut straight to Kasey's heart.

She stopped, panting, and searched for source of the screams.

It has to be a child.

The scream carried above the din of the city. It was close.

Kasey leapt off the fractured sidewalk and into the street. The scream grew louder. Weaving through the traffic, Kasey spotted a sedan with its rear door open. A woman was leaning into the open door, and she seemed to be struggling with something in the back seat.

Kasey ran over to the sedan to find a young mother wrestling with her daughter's car seat. Tears ran down the mother's face as her shaking hands failed to shift the jammed buckle. As the daughter wailed, her mother only grew more frantic. Kasey pulled the mother aside and reached into the car. Grabbing the lock, she fought the mechanism. It wouldn't budge.

Out of time, Kasey whispered, *"Agored!"* The mechanism popped free and Kasey lifted the distraught toddler from the car. Handing the child to her mother, she shouted, "Run! Get away from here now. The city is not safe. Head inland as quickly as you can."

The woman nodded, swiping tears from the child's cheeks.

"Thank you," she stammered.

She turned and bolted down the street, her child clasped against her chest.

Kasey watched her for a moment but tore her eyes away. There was nothing more she could do for her now.

Turning, Kasey ran in the opposite direction. The city was tearing itself apart, but a greater threat still approached. Determined to meet it head on, Kasey made for the bay.

At the traffic light, she turned right. Overhead, the sky was darkening, but it wasn't the setting sun. Boiling black clouds filled the air as they blended with the dense green smoke rising from the city. As they mixed, the clouds took on an emerald hue. Lightning played through the sky as thunder peeled overhead.

The storm was preparing to break, and it was unlike anything Kasey had ever seen. With her heart pounding in her ears at each loping stride, she ran for all she was worth. Her feet pounded against the sidewalk.

The earth shook again. Kasey staggered sideways, almost colliding with a trashcan. Wrapping herself around it, she steadied herself and waited for the tremors to subside.

She looked down the street. A yawning cleft had opened in the face of a towering residential building behind her. Although once a tower full of luxury apartments worth millions, none of that mattered now. The gaping wound in the building's face expanded in a rippling spiderweb of shattered steel and glass. The building swayed as it tore itself apart.

Kasey knew what came next. With the earth shaking underfoot, she darted through the crowd swarming away from its shuddering shadow. Terrified screams followed her up the street.

"The building, it's collapsing," a voice shouted over the chaos.

They should run.

Kasey pushed herself onward. A thunderous crack split the air as the broken building imploded on itself. Risking a glance over her shoulder, Kasey witnessed the dust cloud billowing out from its base.

She had to place more distance between herself and the building. The dust cloud would suffocate her in seconds. She continued to run.

The cloud billowed outward, racing down the street in every direction from the collapsing building. Kasey was already blocks away, but still it surged up the street behind her.

She ran until her side ached. With a deep breath, she looked over her shoulder. The dust's advance was slowing.

That was close. Too close for comfort.

Unfortunately, it wasn't the first building to come down and it wouldn't be the last. For all the destruction that had been visited upon the city, Kasey knew the worst was still to come.

She couldn't believe it had come to this. She'd fought so hard. With every fiber of her being she'd resisted them, but all about her the city told a different story. She had failed.

With more than a decade's warning in her visions, she'd still been powerless to stop the city she called home from being laid low and turned into a wasteland.

The storm broke overhead, and rain bore down on the city in heavy sheets. In moments, she was saturated. Her clothes clung to her as she ran onward.

She wept openly. The heavy tears rolled down her cheeks.

She had given it everything she knew how, and yet it had all come to nothing.

Worse than nothing.

She'd paid a terrible price for that failure. Her heart broke as she thought of John, bleeding out on the floor of the Underpass, her magic powerless to save him, as Akihiro loomed over him. The agony tore into her soul.

Now millions of others would know pain, and there was nothing she could do to stop it. In the distance, a deafening rumble signaled the collapse of another New York City superstructure.

Others would soon follow. They would be either laid low by the tremendous upheaval beneath them, or their collapse from the structural damage caused by the fall of the surrounding buildings. The city was interconnected, and each successive collapse would further weaken the city's urban superstructure.

The earth shook again. This time the seismic tremors were growing closer together. The Shinigami plot was drawing to a close. There was no hope of halting the devastation.

Kasey simply hoped she could do something to save some lives. Something had to be done to mitigate the disaster that was about to occur. The cost of each human death was twofold. Every life was precious, and every death strengthened their foe.

She had no doubt that Akihiro's lingering presence in the city was merely to steal the life force of its inhabitants as they expired. As the carnage unfolded around her, Kasey remembered her earlier visions. In them, the Shinigami's bastion, 432 Park Avenue had stood unmoved and undamaged. Strengthened by whatever preparations Akihiro had laid, it had seemed immune from the seismic activity. As lives by the thousands had been lost, their lifeforce had run up the skyscraper, the building itself taking on a sickly tinge of green.

She'd seen the same transference of energy when John had died at the Shinigami's hand. The thought made her dry heave. The enormity of the Akihiro's callousness still overwhelmed her.

Raising her gaze, she saw her destination come into view. She was at the southernmost point of Manhattan. She ran to the city's edge and grasped the steel rail as she looked out over the bay.

The dark waters had a green tinge to them. Whether it was her imagination or an actual result of the subterranean chaos, she didn't know.

A deafening explosion rang out behind her as the earth reeled beneath her feet. Stumbling, Kasey fell to the ground. Pain shot up her arms as the abrasive surface of the sidewalk skinned both her palms. Kasey was thrown onto her back as the earth shook once more.

This is it. The Shinigami device had been detonated.

If Vida's prediction was accurate, it was already too late. The monolithic detonation far beneath Manhattan would have vaporized the Serpentinite deposits. The vast chasms created would undermine the city and reduce it to ruin.

The earth shook for what felt like an eternity. From flat on her back, Kasey couldn't tell how many buildings had been laid low. Fortunately, those nearest to her managed to stay upright, at least for the time being—likely a result of their distance from Park Avenue. Kasey had run as far as her legs could take her and had reached the southern point of the island in the nick of time.

It wasn't a bid to escape her fate. She intended to stand against what would come next.

As the tremors ceased, she struggled to her feet. Her body roared its pained protest at the abuse it had suffered over the recent weeks.

Not much longer now. It will all be over soon.

As she teetered on her feet, she grabbed the steel rail for support. She looked over the rail into the murky depths of the bay. The water was already receding. The inky black waters rolled away from Manhattan like it was low tide. The water couldn't escape the city quick enough and as Kasey watched it recede, she knew Vida was right.

Damn him. He's always right.

The seconds ticked inexorably by, each one coming and going as the city burned to ashes behind her. She couldn't worry about that now. The worst still lay ahead.

Then she saw it. At first, against the horizon, it was almost indiscernible among the angry storm clouds that blended seamlessly with the sea beneath. As it rolled toward Kasey, she could see it clearer and clearer with each passing moment. The wall of water was almost a hundred feet high, racing toward the city.

This was the implacable, crushing conclusion to the Shinigami plot.

The immense wall of water would be the end of New York City. It would sweep through the structurally weakened cityscape doing incalculable damage. Anyone on the street would be drowned or battered to death by the debris.

It was even larger than Kasey had imagined. As the wall of water rolled toward her, she realized the impossibility of her task.

What was one woman against such a wave? It was a tsunami, the likes of which the East Coast had never seen.

Kasey raised her hands and summoned her magic. Anything she could do to slow the tide would save lives. It wasn't a matter of if the wave would strike the city, but simply how far it would reach. Every block it rolled through, it would claim thousands, if not tens of thousands of lives.

The sting of her defeat was bitter, but if she could rob Akihiro of even a single life force it was worth it to her.

She had seen too much suffering and felt too much pain to let another person endure the heartache she had struggled with every day. As the wave closed, Kasey felt a vibration in her pocket. It was her phone.

Somehow with all the damage the city had suffered, her cellular service was still working. As the wave plunged toward her, Kasey ripped out her phone. The display read *Mom*.

Saying goodbye was more than Kasey could bear. She rejected the call. The cell display flashed back to its desktop.

It read 15th of December 2017 5:35 PM.

Kasey looked up. As the wave descended, so did a thick gray-green mist. The familiar embrace of her prescience enshrouded her as her vision closed.

CHAPTER 2

Kasey's eyes snapped open. An intermittent beeping drew her attention to a monitor next to her bed. On the green and black display, a thin line bounced up and down as it traversed the screen.

She was flat on her back. Much of the room beyond was concealed by a lime curtain drawn around her bed. It took her a moment to separate her current situation from the vision she had just witnessed.

Sitting up, she rubbed her weary eyes.

The aging yet sterile decor told her she was in the Administorum in the Arcane Council's headquarters. She had been here before. The last thing she could remember was Akihiro's flight from the Council Chambers and his escape into downtown Manhattan.

What had happened?

More importantly, how long had she been here? Her vision was a clear warning that Akihiro was on the loose and would soon bear out his deadly plot. After everything that had happened, she was locked in a race against time. She was facing a literal deadline. One that New York City would not survive.

If she couldn't stop him in time, then Akihiro would wipe out the city. New York, along with much of the eastern seaboard of the United States, would never be the same again.

She knew the council would still be reeling from the revelation that the Chancellor was an imposter. The Ainsleys were gone, it was difficult to believe. Arthur Ainsley had been dead for almost a year, but John's death had come at Akihiro's hand as the Shinigami fled the Council Chambers. The memory filled her with both anger and pain.

Kasey forced it from her mind.

Beside her bed on a rolling trolley sat a breakfast tray displaying an untouched set of bacon and eggs. Normally she would have attacked it hungrily, but she was looking for something else.

Resting beside the untouched breakfast was her phone. Kasey grabbed it and checked the display. Low battery.

Of course. Why should I expect anything else?

She thumbed past the warning to bring up the main screen.

Her heart skipped a beat, as her fingers tightened around her phone.

15th of December 2017 7:10 AM.

Oh, no.

Her heart began to race. The attack was today. In less than ten hours, New York City would be no more.

She had no time to waste.

Throwing her legs over the edge of the bed, Kasey lowered her feet to the ground. She tore off the heart rate monitor. The machine started to beep loudly as it came off.

Ignoring the noise, Kasey reached for the curtain. Tugging it back a little, she peered around the edge. She was the only patient in the room. On the chair beside her lay her clothes. They appeared to have been laundered and now sat cleanly pressed and ready to wear.

She ripped off her hospital robe and pulled on her jeans and T-shirt, followed by her socks and boots. Over the back of the chair hung her black leather jacket. It was battered and scuffed from the chaos in the Council Chambers.

In one deft motion, Kasey pulled on the jacket, relishing the smooth feel of the jacket against her skin. It was December, and the temperature out would only continue to plummet. Slipping her phone into her pocket, she pushed the curtain back and made for the exit. No sooner had she cleared the hospital room then she came face-to-face with a nurse.

"Miss Chase, what are you doing up?" The nurse asked, her voice a high-pitched whine. Raising both hands she attempted to shepherd Kasey back the way she had come. "You need bed rest. The Chancellor asked us to let you rest as long as you needed. He was very clear you were not to be disturbed."

Kasey scrunched up her face at the mention of the Chancellor. "The Chancellor is dead, my dear. An impostor has been masquerading in Arthur's place but rest assured, neither the imposter nor Arthur himself would have cared about my well-being."

The nurse placed a hand on Kasey's shoulder, "I'm not talking about Arthur, dear. I'm talking about Chancellor Sanders. In the wake of what happened in the council, they have made him acting Chancellor of the Arcane Council. It was he that insisted we let you rest as long as you needed."

"Sanders is the Chancellor?" Kasey asked, sweeping her hair back behind her ear.

Some good news at last.

"Yes, dear. The surviving council members voted unanimously."

"Well, that should make things a little easier. Let's hope they have retained their unified front. We're going to need it."

With that, Kasey ducked around the nurse and headed for the Administorum's door.

"Where are you going?" the nurse called after her.

"Out. I'm off to see the Chancellor." Kasey paused to look over her shoulder. "Where is he?"

The nurse hesitated. "He should be in the sanctum, I would think. The Council has been holed up down there for days."

Kasey strode past the admissions desk, ignoring the staff member on duty there.

If this is the last day of my life, I'm not going to spend it in a hospital.

Kasey picked up her pace until she checked herself out. She knew from her previous visit that the Administorum was located on the tenth subbasement of the council headquarters. If she wanted Sanders he would be in the Council Chambers below.

Reaching the bank of elevators, she found one waiting. She pressed the button and the doors parted to allow her entry. The car was empty. She dashed inside and pressed the button for the twenty-fifth floor.

The doors closed and the elevator plunged downward. It only took a few moments to reach the twenty-fifth floor. As soon as the doors parted, she stepped out of the elevator, back in the now familiar lobby before the Arcane Council's Courtroom and Sanctum. The metal detectors were still in place, but the lobby was empty except for a cohort of six ADI agents who stood before the door.

A rather stout agent at the head of the group called out to her, "Miss. You can't come in here. It's an open court. The council is in session. For security reasons, we need you to step back into the elevator and be about your business."

Kasey continued straight toward them. "Where is Sanders? Is he in there? I need to speak with him at once."

"Miss, as I was saying, you can't enter," the agent said, bristling.

The agent to his right laid a hand on his shoulder and whispered in his ear.

Kasey was close enough to overhear him.

"That's her. That's Kasey Chase," the agent whispered excitedly.

The stout agent looked her up and down, then his posture relaxed. "Ah, Miss Chase, my apologies. I'm sure the Chancellor would be eager to see you are back on your feet. Come on through. I'll announce you."

Kasey passed through the metal detector. It was silent. She wondered where her gun had got to. She hadn't seen it since she was arrested in Central Park.

The stout agent gestured for her to follow him.

She slipped between the other agents as they parted to allow her passage. The stout lead agent made his way to the heavy oak doors and pushed them open.

The court's gallery was empty. The council's raised lectern was still a battered wreckage dominating one end of the chamber.

The prosecution and the accused's tables had been removed. In the space sat a single table with eight chairs around it, five of them occupied. Kasey noted Sanders sat at the head of the table. Along each edge of the table sat two council members she had seen previously.

Only five of the council had survived.

One of the councilmen, a balding man to Sander's right, had spoken in Kasey's defense. His efforts had allowed Kasey the time she needed to agitate and reveal Akihiro as the Master of the Shinigami.

He studied Kasey with one eye, the right side of his face hidden beneath a bandage. Kasey was relieved to see he had survived the encounter with Akihiro. She may not have known his name, but she was grateful for the role he had played, albeit unintentionally.

Sanders rose out of his chair. "Kasey, it's good to see you're back on your feet. How are you feeling?"

"I've felt better." Kasey strode over to the table. "I've definitely felt a lot worse too, all things considered. May I sit?"

"By all means." Sanders pointed to the seat Kasey stood behind. "Truth be told, you couldn't have come at a better time."

"You don't know the half of it," Kasey answered, sliding into the seat. "We're out of time."

The councilwoman at Kasey's left turned to her. "What do you mean?"

Sanders held up his hand. "Before we get into it, I'd like to introduce you to our sitting council members. I know you have appeared before the council previously, but never like this. If we are to present a united front against Akihiro, you should get to know who is in the trench beside you. You aren't alone in this fight anymore. There may not be many of us left, but we will see it through."

Kasey nodded, as she wrung her hands under the table. "Sure. I've got to say, it's a lot nicer to sit at the table with you then to appear before you on the bench. Don't expect an apology for my past, folks. I've been fighting for my life."

Sanders raised his hand to stop her. "There is no apology needed, Kasey. Like I said, I just want you to know who is with you. Akihiro may have held Arthur's seat, but these are four of the finest witches and wizards I've ever met. They would lay down their lives, for you, for me, for our community."

"That's no small claim, Sanders," Kasey said with a tired smirk. "It may yet be required of each of us."

"Indeed, it may." Sanders pointed to the wizard at Kasey's left. He was middle aged, with a slender face and wrinkled brow. His gray hair had been cropped short. "This is Vincent Kane. Vincent is our Master of Medicines and Maladies. As part of his duties on the Council, he oversees the Administorum along with our research division."

Kasey smiled. "My thanks for your care, Vincent. Your staff have been most attentive."

"You are most welcome, Miss Chase. After all you've done, we couldn't have you die of exhaustion and dehydration."

"Quite," Sanders replied, moving on to the woman at his right. The woman was older than Kasey, perhaps in her late fifties, though her freshly dyed sandy blonde hair made it difficult to tell. Her big hairdo reminded Kasey of movies she'd seen from the eighties. The woman's eyes locked with Kasey. Her gaze wasn't nearly as warm as Vincent's. "Kasey, this is Stacey Lender. Stacey serves as our Keeper of Knowledge. The archives are her domain. Few understand our history better than Stacey."

That explains it. We trashed her precious archives in our escape.

"What's left of it anyway," Stacey replied, letting out a lingering sigh. "We lost years of priceless manuscripts during your escapades in the archives."

Kasey didn't bat an eyelash. "If we'd let the ADI catch us, we'd both be dead, and an impostor would still be leading this august body. The damage done will pale compared to what Akihiro has in store."

"What's done is done," Sanders interjected. He turned his attention to the bandaged wizard at his left. "This is Michael Rosenberg. Michael is responsible for our judicial system. He oversees legislative efforts, our court procedures, and ensures balance between the heavy hand of the ADI and our penal system."

His interference in her trial now made sense. Several times, Rosenberg had silenced Akihiro to ensure Kasey could speak her peace.

"I appreciate your attempts to moderate my trial, Mr. Rosenberg," Kasey said. "Your interdiction allowed me the chance to unmask the pretender before he knew what was coming."

Michael nodded. "As overwhelming as the evidence might have been, Miss Chase, justice must be impartial. It was no more than you deserved, and far less, if half of what Sanders has told us is true."

Sanders gestured to the final counselor, seated at Kasey's right. The stern woman was broad-shouldered with frizzy black hair. "This is Helena Alexopolous. Helena is our Minister for Education. She oversees the Academy of Magic and is responsible for the teaching of our rising generation. Her mastery of the arcane is the envy of our community."

The witch waved away the compliment. "You are too kind, Chancellor, though I fear my skills pale beside your own. Nonetheless, I will give my all to put an end to the pretender. He must pay for what he has done to our companions. Such callous violence cannot go unpunished."

"I agree entirely. Akihiro must be stopped. No matter the cost," Kasey said. "Many have already paid the ultimate price. John Ainsley, his father the Chancellor—both of them are victims in this. They are not alone. Dozens of other people have found themselves in the Shinigami's crosshairs and lost their lives. Members of the magical community and normals, none are safe. My own precinct has suffered terribly for our role in wiping out his followers. I only wish we'd got to him sooner."

"As do I, but wishing won't make it so. We must focus on the task at hand, putting an end to his machinations once and for all," Vincent said, leaning forward in his chair.

"You said we are out of time, Miss Chase. What exactly did you mean?" Councilwoman Lender asked. "And how did you come to be in possession of such information? I was led to believe you've been in a coma since your appearance here in this chamber. How is it that you are privy to the Shinigami's plot?"

Kasey grit her teeth. The Councilwoman's disdain was understandable, but it was misplaced. After everything Kasey had done, she expected more.

"I would have thought by now I would have earned the benefit of the doubt. After all, without me, you would all still be ignoring the traitor in your midst—as you would his plot to destroy the city, which is as real as any of us sitting around this table. You can continue to second-guess me, Councilwoman, but when it comes to the Shinigami and their plot, you're all playing a game of catch up that we can scarcely afford to lose."

"Benefit of the doubt, yes," the Councilwoman replied, "but this body has safely governed the affairs of the magical community in this country for centuries. You haven't maintained our world by hurtling blindly into the face of every threat that's reared its ugly head. Akihiro and his minions are a very real danger, but they are not first such, nor shall they be the last. We will all have a say in how we respond to the danger they present. I asked how you came to be in possession of this information?"

"I heard the question," Kasey answered, locking eyes with Lender. "You were at my hearing, right? I knew Akihiro had stepped up his plot the same way. I knew that Arthur was dead, and that Akihiro had killed Theo Getz. I saw it in a vision. I'm prescient. It's my gift, or curse. I guess it depends how you look at it."

"Prescient?" Lender said with a laugh. "I knew you claimed to be prescient in court, I suppose I had thought it was merely part of your theatrics, part of your plot to uncover Akihiro."

"I assure you it's very real, counselor," Kasey said, leaning over the table as she stretched out her hand. "Take my hand, and I'll prove it. Though I must warn you, I have little control over exactly what I see. Past, the soon to be present, or the future. It is seldom pleasant, but what do you say, counselor, would you like to know how you die?"

Lender recoiled. "Uh, I'm..."

Kasey smiled at the counselor's discomfort. "As I was saying, I saw it in a vision this morning. Hence why I came here immediately. We don't have time for pointless semantics. Akihiro is on the move. We have to stop him now, before it is too late."

"Easy, Kasey, we're all on the same side here," Sanders said. "You must understand, it's difficult for others to understand what it must be like to have your abilities. The gift is so rare, many still think they the stuff of old wives' tales."

"If only. It certainly would have made my life simpler," Kasey said. "People seem to forget, I didn't ask for any of this."

Rosenberg cleared his throat. "You may not have asked for it, but all things considered, we are fortunate that you do. Let's not squander the opportunity it affords us. Tell us, Kasey, what did you see?"

"I saw the attack on the city," Kasey said. "The earth shook as the city tore itself apart. Building after building collapsed. I ran for my life as the dust clouds choked the life out of everyone who walked the streets. I made it to the bay in time to meet the tsunami that the earthquake had brought. If that attack occurs, millions will die. That is Akihiro's plot. He would destroy the city, tear the heart out of our country, and siphon the life force from those slaughtered in the attack."

She paused to allow her words to sink in.

The council sat speechless, except for Sanders who leaned back in his chair.

"We knew that before, Kasey. What else did you see this morning?"

Kasey sucked in a deep breath. "I saw the date. We're out of time, Sanders. The attack is today and I have no idea how to stop it."

CHAPTER 3

The room was silent. The counselors looked from Kasey to Sanders, and back to Kasey, but none of them seemed to be able to find their words.

Sanders straightened in his chair. "Today, Kasey? Are you certain?"

"Yes, the tsunami struck the city just after 5:30PM, on the 15th of December. I know I have been unconscious for some time, but unless I'm mistaken, today is the 15th. We are out of time. Akihiro will attack the city today."

"So soon..." Sanders replied. "I had hoped for more time."

"We have none. We must take them today, before it's too late." Kasey struck the table with her fist. "We must gather our forces and storm their headquarters before they can detonate the weapon."

"Their headquarters? You know where they are?" Helena asked. "Why have we waited?"

"Yes and no," Sanders answered. "We suspect the new construction at 432 Park Avenue to be at the heart of their plan, but we were not certain. We didn't want to warn them that we knew of their location. If Akihiro escapes the city, who knows what destruction he will wreak. We must ensure that he meets his end here. Every step of the way he has been ahead of us, planning and plotting this massacre. More than a year of his life was dedicated to this ruse, and never once have we had the upper hand, until we revealed him before the court. We were fortunate then, but we won't get lucky twice. If we are to stop him now, it will require us to plan our assault carefully. If we fail, all will be lost."

"That is true, but it's time to act." Kasey rose from the table. "We have only hours left, and precious few of them at that."

Sanders looked up at her. "I know, Kasey, but with care we can raise our chance for success. The deck may be stacked against us, but we have not been idly waiting for you to wake. We have allies who will stand with us. With your aid, we may yet have more."

"And we must put the evacuation protocols into place immediately," Councilwoman Lender interjected. "The more people we can get out of the city, the better. Eight hours is less than we need but it will have to do."

Kasey slid back into her seat. "An evacuation won't work. I saw the effects in my vision. If we signal an evacuation, there will be riots and looting. The bridges and tunnels will be gridlocked, and the city will panic. There will be anarchy. Moreover, we'll be sending a signal loud and clear that we know that today is the day they strike. The evacuation order might be exactly what causes Akihiro to act in the first place."

"Hard to say which comes first, the chicken or the egg. The evacuation order might set off the attack, but without it, if the attack occurs, millions will die. Some of whom could have been saved if we'd acted first," Rosenberg answered.

Kasey frowned. "If we know it won't work, what purpose will it serve other than to warn our enemy?"

"Understood," Sanders replied. "We'll hold off on the evacuation order until our assault is under way. By then, it won't matter that he knows, and it may still save lives."

"I can live with that." Kasey pushed her hair back behind her ear. "So, you mentioned an assault. That's an idea I can get behind. What's the plan?"

Sanders continued, "Before we can assault anything, we will need to clear a path. New York City has not taken kindly to the discovery of witches and wizards living in their midst."

Oh, no. Kasey sank her head into her hands. She had forgotten the manner of Akihiro's escape. He'd tortured his way down Broadway, butchering innocents and police in full view of a street crowded with witnesses. His disciples had been heavily armed, but he'd used his magic on purpose. He had no doubt been aware of the chaos that would ensue.

That moment—the sight of a wizard torturing innocents with magic as he marauded through the city—had been captured by hundreds. The footage will have been played around the world. The World of Magic was no longer a secret.

"How bad is it?" Kasey asked.

"Worse than we expected," Sanders said. "Our kind are in hiding. The city is paranoid and on edge. We've kept them at bay and above ground, but only because they don't know what to look for. Anyone that displays arcane power above ground is getting mobbed. If we are to move out in force, we are going to need allies. We are going to need help from the police to clear a path and lock down the target site. Otherwise we're going to get swarmed and innocents will die. They are ignorant, but they are innocent, nonetheless. Do you think you can secure help from the Ninth Precinct?"

The thought of seeing Bishop again brought a smile to Kasey's face. That smile soon deflated as she recalled why they had lost contact with the Ninth Precinct in the first place: the ADI's media campaign of misinformation had driven a wedge between her and her former employer.

Kasey and Sanders had been the most wanted fugitives in the Tristate area.

"I would, but I doubt the Ninth Precinct are going to listen to me after that smear campaign the ADI ran," she said. "The Ninth probably still thinks I murdered an apartment building full of senior citizens. I'm hardly employee of the month right now."

"You don't have to worry about the Ninth Precinct, Kasey," Sanders began. "As soon as we had control of the Council back from Akihiro, we began working on the damage he'd done to our reputations. There may still be some skeptics among the public, but we've issued retractions of the claims that he made. We've also found footage of the Night Crew operating from that stash house. The truth is out, Kasey, and in time we should be entirely free of those accusations."

"I hear you, but that hardly guarantees a warm reception. They may not think I'm a murderer, but I doubt they will take kindly to me being a witch either. All things considered."

Sanders nodded. "You're not wrong. You know your colleagues at the Ninth better than we do. How much you tell them is up to you, but if we want to move out in force, we are going to need their assistance keeping the public in check and locking down the target. Without their help, it will be chaos. We can't afford to take the chance."

Kasey tapped her fingers on the table. "Alright. Let's say we succeed in getting them on our side. What is the plan then? How are we tackling the assault? We're going to need a concrete plan. Do we have any idea how many acolytes Akihiro has at his disposal? What kind of forces are we up against?"

"He had at least thirty followers when he fled the Arcane Council. We know they are heavily armed and that they are fortifying their position. Unfortunately, their numbers are also growing."

"Growing, how?" Kasey clenched her fist, her knuckles turning white.

Rosenberg looked at Kasey through his one good eye. "The day after Akihiro was revealed for who he truly is, we noticed more wizards than usual not showing up for work throughout the Council offices. At first, we thought it was shock at the Chancellor's death, or fear of what the public might do if their secret was discovered, but the numbers continued to grow. Day by day, it became more noticeable. Their absence hindered our efforts to reorganize the affairs of our community. I informed Sanders of them, and that is when we realized what was happening."

"What was happening?" Kasey asked, almost grinding her teeth.

"Some of our people have defected to Akihiro," Sanders replied with an exasperated sigh. "I have agents watching Park Avenue. People have been seen trickling into the building. At first, we thought they were his original acolytes coming and going, but the numbers are increasing, and we've begun running the identities of those we see entering the building. They are ours, or at least they were. It seems Akihiro is growing in popularity."

Kasey's heart sank and her blood boiled as Sanders spoke. She had spent so long fighting against Akihiro, and her own kind were willingly joining him.

"Why would anyone side with that monster?" Kasey shouted. "He's going to destroy the city."

"I don't imagine he's leading with that as the party line," Lender chimed in.

Kasey smoldered.

"No," Sanders agreed. "But his promise of a prolonged life certainly has an allure. Not to mention the protection he's offering against the public. Our people are scared, and they know Akihiro won't hesitate to harm a normal. I suppose they feel safe, as warped as it is. It seems to be working, though. Akihiro is welcoming them with open arms."

"How many of our kind have joined him?" Kasey asked softly, her stomach churning.

"We have no way of knowing," Sanders replied. "Many are absent. I'm sure that most of them are simply hiding at home, waiting for the storm to pass. We've seen at least two dozen that we know of, though. It could be more."

"With more joining him every moment," Kasey said. "It will grow worse if he succeeds. New York will be gutted. In the wake of such a display of power, others will come. For the first time in centuries, we would have civil war among those who survive. It would be catastrophic, and that's before the normals retaliate. They won't care that it was Akihiro that caused the devastation. We'll all be blamed for it."

"We can't allow it to come to that," Helena interjected. "That would set us back centuries, and the middle ages were kind to no one, witch or normal alike. Everyone suffered. We must stop him here and now."

"Agreed," Kasey said. "So, we get the police on our side and we hit him with everything we have."

"You're the one who has seen it in a vision, Kasey," Vincent turned his gaze to her. "You've also had the most dealings with the Shinigami. What would you suggest?"

Kasey leaned back in her chair. At least, finally, the Council was taking her seriously. "We root them out. All of them, root and stem. Today."

"How would you do it?" Vincent asked.

Kasey folded her arms. "Frontal assault. Akihiro doesn't know what we know. He expects to detonate the weapon and take us by surprise. If the police will cooperate, we'll have them seal the neighborhood for five blocks in every direction. We go in hard and fast, ram-raid the lobby, and unload directly into the building. We'll split into two teams. One team will head down into the subbasement in search for Akihiro's weapon. The other will sweep upward through the building, clearing any resistance as we go. I know Akihiro will be watching the carnage from the observation deck. If we can get aerial support, we can have tactical teams insert from above and sweep downward. If we can't stop Akihiro in time, we'll bring the building down on top of them. Take out the weapon before it can be detonated."

"No half-measures," Sanders replied. "Many will die."

"If we hesitate, it could be millions," Kasey said, and her thoughts flittered over her vision. "How many agents can we muster for the assault?"

Sanders scratched his head. "I had hoped for more time. Our numbers have been thinned. We buried some good men as a result of Akihiro's flight. Others are still recovering from injuries. Some have disappeared. We can probably muster thirty or forty agents on short notice."

"That few? I was hoping for more," Kasey ran her fingers through her hair.

"Me too," Sanders replied. "Beggars can't be choosers, though. It's all we have. We'll have more if the police side with us."

"We don't have long," Kasey replied. "If they aren't with us now, they may never be."

"I'll make a call while you are at the precinct." Sanders pulled a phone out of his pocket and slid it across the table. "If you're successful, call me, and we'll set a time and place to rendezvous for the assault."

Kasey grabbed the phone off the table as she stood up. "Understood. I'll take a run at Chief West and see if I can't garner their support. Wish me luck."

Sanders smiled. "I think I speak for all of us when I say, we wish you luck."

Kasey nodded. "Thanks."

She turned for the door but paused. Looking over her shoulder, she said, "All things considered, this went much better than my previous visits. I think I'm starting to grow on you. Even you, Lender, though you do a great job of hiding it."

Lender scoffed.

Kasey turned for the door, her smile spreading as she let herself out of the Council Chambers. It was high time she returned to the Ninth Precinct. How would her former colleagues react to her return? She'd been painted as a fugitive and a murderer. Kasey only hoped they gave her a chance to explain before tossing her in a cell.

CHAPTER 4

Kasey pushed open the Ninth Precinct's heavy steel doors. It was a relief to be off the street. The windchill was making the wintry weather bite all the more. Kasey had been ready for the cold, but the chaos had caught her off guard. Roving packs of citizens scoured the city like lynch mobs. As soon as she'd spotted the first making its way down Broadway toward her, she'd hailed a cab.

She crossed the lobby of the Ninth Precinct, heading toward the bank of elevators.

An officer stepped into her path and raised his hand to bring her to a halt. "Miss Chase, I'm going to need you to wait here."

The barrel-chested officer was no stranger to her.

Kasey sighed. "Morales, what's going on? I need to see Bishop and the Chief. Where are they?"

"West is in his office. Bishop, I'm not sure. She's probably in the bullpen. I'll page them and have her come down."

"No need, Morales, I'll find her." Kasey stepped around him.

He shuffled sideways. "Sorry, Kasey, I can't let you through."

Kasey raised an eyebrow. "Since when?"

"Since the chief suspended you last week," Morales replied. "You are a wanted fugitive."

Kasey felt her pulse quicken as her cheeks flushed red. "That was a misunderstanding. I didn't do anything."

"That's not for me to decide," Morales answered. "Until the Chief clears you, you can't freely wander the station. Grab a seat. I'll have Bishop come straight down."

Kasey looked over Morales' shoulder. The bank of elevators was right there, and she had no time for this. The city had no time for this.

"I know that look, Kasey. You might be a bad ass, but if you try to jump me in the middle of the station, you're just going to make things worse. So just grab a seat and relax. Bishop will be right down."

He was right, as much as she disliked that. She strode over to a bench seat and flopped down. She let out a sigh.

The city is going to be leveled and I'm a prisoner in my own precinct. Well, today is just off to a brilliant start.

Morales strode over to the lobby's reception desk and picked up a phone. "Yeah, this is Morales. Can you find Bishop for me? I have a guest in the lobby. I think she's going to want to come down."

Kasey tapped her foot while she considered her next move. She had hoped for a better reception; her suspension would complicate matters further. West would be even less inclined to listen to her. She also wanted to see Vida. He had been the first to uncover the true nature of the Shinigami's plot. She hoped that by now he had an idea of what type of weapon the Shinigami might be using. If they could figure that out, they might be able to disarm it before it could detonate beneath the city.

"Kasey!" a voice shouted.

Kasey tuned to see Bishop striding across the lobby. Bishop had her blonde hair tied back, and her pantsuit was pristine and pressed as usual. She was smiling from ear-to-ear. In light of her usually stern demeanor, it was a welcome change.

At least someone is glad to see me.

Kasey leapt to her feet and headed for Bishop.

Without hesitation, Bishop threw her arms around Kasey. "It's good to see you, Kasey. When we didn't hear from you, we feared the worst."

"Feared the worst? I'm told West suspended me," Kasey said, returning the embrace.

Bishop let go of her. "That was before. You had the FBI running ads about you, Kasey. You and Sanders made the most wanted list. We didn't want to believe it, but it put West in an unenviable position. He couldn't have you on the active duty roster and the FBI's most wanted list at the same time. Don't stress about it, though. I'm sure he'll restore your status once he knows you're back. You are back aren't you, Kasey?"

"Sort of." Kasey jammed her hands into her jacket pockets. "Is there somewhere quiet we can talk?"

"The bullpen is kind of crazy. Let's head downstairs. At least we never have to fight anyone for a seat in the morgue." Bishop nodded toward the stairs.

Kasey followed her into the staircase.

Free from eavesdroppers, Kasey asked, "Is it really that bad?"

Bishop turned to look at Kasey. "What do you mean? Is it that bad? Have you been outside? The city is in an uproar. The government is talking about instituting martial law. Things are out of control. How do you not know this? Kasey, where have you been?"

"Underground and most recently unconscious, at least for the past forty-eight hours. My trip here was the first time I've seen the sun in days."

Bishop's eyes widened. "What happened?"

Kasey kept walking, "Let's get to the morgue. Vida will want to know too, and time is short, so I'd rather not repeat myself, if that's okay?"

"Sure, no worries. I'm just glad you're alright."

Together, they made their way down the hall and into the morgue. Vida was standing at the whiteboard, scribbling away.

He looked over his shoulder. "Kasey! It's so good to see you."

"You too, Vida." She came up to peer over his shoulder. "What are you working on?"

Vida put down the marker. "I've just been looking into the building at Park Avenue. I'm trying to work out how long it will take the Shinigami to drill down and detonate their weapon. I want to know how long we have to stop them."

"I can help you there," Kasey said, dropping onto a stool. "We have ten hours, give or take."

"Ten hours?" Vida spluttered. "What? That soon? How do you know?"

"A vision?" Bishop asked, grabbing a chair for herself.

"Yes. I saw it this morning. If we don't stop the Shinigami by six pm, the city as we know it will cease to exist. Millions will die."

Vida sank into his chair. "Well, I guess that answers that. I've got to say, Kasey, I've missed you, but I haven't missed the doom and gloom that seems to follow you, like your own personal storm cloud."

"Alright Kasey, we're all here," Bishop said. "Why don't you bring us up to speed with what's been going on? We need to be on the same page if we're going to have a chance of stopping this. Why don't you start with where you went when you disappeared from the station? One moment I was talking to you and Sanders, the next you were just gone."

Kasey nodded. "You're going to get the condensed version, okay? We don't have time for everything that has happened. It's been a hectic few weeks and frankly, it would take all day to cover it all."

"The abridged version is fine, Kasey," Bishop said. "Give us the highlights."

"Alright." Kasey swiveled on her stool. "So, when you helped us escape from Council Headquarters, we knew that you'd bought us some time but that it wouldn't last forever. Sooner or later, the ADI would come and squeeze West until you gave us up. We couldn't have that, so we slipped out of the station and made a run for it. We figured the less you knew about our plans, the less they could lean on you. We wanted to give you plausible deniability."

"Fair enough," Bishop said, leaning forward. "What happened next?"

"We went on the run. The ADI harried us everywhere we went. We couldn't speak to anyone we knew, and we were quickly running out of cash. We knew we had to turn the tables on the Shinigami, but we seemed to be getting further and further from being able to do anything. With Akihiro and his Shinigami in control of the council, we were losing ground fast. That's when we decided to rob the Night Crew."

"You do realize how insane that sounds?" Vida asked. "Do you know how many bodies have come through this very room because of them? They are ruthless."

"I know. It was Sanders' idea. We needed resources and we didn't want to harm any innocents. So, we hit them instead. We raided one of their stash-houses. We destroyed as much of their drugs as we could on the way through, and when we reached their safe, we stole enough cash to keep us going and burnt the rest to the ground."

"How much is enough?" Bishop asked.

"Three million," Kasey replied, "give or take. We must have burned almost double that. There was no way for us to transport that much cash."

Bishop's eyes went wide. "There was ten million in cash? No wonder we are struggling to make a dint in their operation. With that much money on hand, they can hire an army."

"Agreed. Based on the intel we gathered, they have other stash houses located throughout the city. There was enough firepower there to start a small war. We took out a lot of them on our way through, but it's a spit in the ocean. If we survive the Shinigami plot, there will be a reckoning."

"Where is the money now?" Bishop asked.

"Gone. We used a chunk of it to hire some help against the Shinigami. We lost some when a Night Crew hit man tracked me to my hotel, and the rest, well, I'm not sure. Sander had it and I haven't really had a chance to talk to him about it. It didn't seem like our most pressing issue to be honest."

"Fair enough," Vida said. "Ignoring that whole Night Crew hit man part, which we will talk about later, what happened next?"

"We were going after Akihiro and his Shinigami but we needed more intel. We needed to know where he was if we were to be able to take him out. So, I met with John to discover where Akihiro might be hiding. After all, he was masquerading as Arthur Ainsley, so if anyone was going to know something, it would be John. Unfortunately, the meeting was a trap. The ADI followed John to Central Park and caught me. I put up a fight, but there was just too many of them. I was taken into custody by the ADI."

"How did you survive that?" Bishop scowled. "I would have thought Akihiro would have killed you."

Kasey nodded. "He certainly wanted to, but he needed to know where Sanders was, so he was trying to leverage me with pressure from the ADI. If he'd had known that I knew his true identity, I'm sure I would have been dead in my cell."

"So, you didn't tip your hand?" Bishop nodded appreciatively. "Good call."

"I thought so. It didn't do me a lot of good though. They dragged me before the council and tried to prosecute me for everything that had happened over the last few weeks—breaking into the Arcane Council, trying to abduct the Chancellor, vandalizing the city. Everything. There were enough charges for a capital sentence if I was convicted."

"How did you get out of that?" Vida asked, rocking on his seat.

"At great cost," Kasey replied, scratching at the nape of her neck. "Sanders came through for me. He slipped me a key for my cuffs and during the trial I ditched them and went after Akihiro. I shattered his illusion in the middle of the crowded courtroom. The world saw him for who he truly was, and they turned on him. During the carnage, he killed a number of members of the Arcane Council and ran for his life."

Bishop's eyes widened. "So, you dislodged him from the Council. Nice work. Without the ADI backing him, it will be easier to bring him down."

"That's what we thought," Kasey said, her eyes starting to water at the memory. "Turns out, he still has plenty of acolytes willing to do his bidding. We hunted him through the Underpass but when we confronted him, his minions were there. There was a firefight, and during it he..." Kasey took a shuddering breath. "He killed John and made his escape."

"John is dead?" Bishop whispered. "Kasey, I'm so sorry."

Kasey shook her head. Thinking of John made her heart ache in so many ways. "I can't talk about that, please. Not now."

"Okay, Kasey, what happened next?" Bishop rested her hand on Kasey's knee and gave her a small smile.

"Akihiro made it out and butchered his way through lower Manhattan. I'm sure you've seen the footage. That was him and his cronies. With his identity revealed, he wanted to plunge the city into as much chaos as possible, so he outed the World of Magic in an effort to tie up the council's resources while he destroys the city."

"It's proved effective," Bishop replied. "We've been flat out trying to keep people in check. The footage of Akihiro attacking innocent bystanders was everywhere. It played on every channel, and it's all over the web. People don't' know how to respond to it. Some think he's a one of a kind, some sort of government engineered super soldier. Others swear its magic. One thing is clear though—he murdered a dozen innocents on prime-time TV. The city knows it's a threat. Anyone displaying extra-normal abilities is being hunted. You need to make sure that your people lay low, Kasey. This may yet blow over."

"We can't keep doing that, Bishop," Kasey shook her head. "We only have hours to stop them, and there's not going to be anything discreet about the fight that is to come. The Arcane Council knows the game is up. Too much has happened, and soon the world is going to understand the truth. The council is done hiding. If they don't deal with Akihiro, he'll destroy the city. What do you think that will do? A wizard taking out the Tristate area. It will plunge us into a civil war. Normals versus wizards. It will be a bloodbath."

"Okay, so what's their plan?" Vida asked.

"Direct assault, and they want the precinct's help. We need to talk to West."

Bishop rose from her chair. "No time like the present. What are you going to tell him?"

Kasey got to her feet and stretched both arms. "The truth, and as much of it as it takes to convince him how dire the threat is."

"I'm coming with you," Vida said, standing up. "We've seen the Shinigami's work close up, and I know what's going on at Park Avenue. I'm sure that together, we can get him on our side."

The tears brimming in Kasey's eyes slid down her cheeks. She dabbed them away. "It is good to see you both again. In the past few weeks, there were days when I didn't think I would."

Bishop wrapped her arm around Kasey's shoulder. "Us, too. I'm glad we were wrong. Now, let's go see the chief."

CHAPTER 5

K asey studied Chief West. He sat back in his chair; his arms crossed firmly across his chest. His lips were drawn tight. Black bags were visible beneath his eyes, his expression utterly unreadable.

Across the desk from West sat Bishop and Vida, occupying the two chairs. Kasey stood behind them, leaning on the chair backs.

Chief West frowned. "So, what you're telling me is that the reason you've been absent the past few weeks is, you have been working to take down a mad wizard that is trying to destroy the city? Your stint on the FBI's most wanted list was as a result of a misinformation campaign they had run against you, and that if I don't rally the forces of the Ninth Precinct behind you and perform a direct assault on a luxury residential tower, then the entire city is going to be destroyed by the end of the day? Does that about sum things up?"

Kasey stood up a little straighter and ran her hand through a hair. "When you say it like that, it does sound a little crazy. But the thing is, it's also the truth. So, let's get specific, which part are you having trouble with?"

"Let's try all of it," West replied.

Kasey went to open her mouth, but Bishop cut her off. "Chief, I know it sounds far-fetched, but you've seen the footage of the

Broadway attack. How can you explain that, if not for magic? Those poor souls were suspended in the air and tortured, before being brutally murdered. That man is a wizard. The same powers he was using to hurt all those innocent people, are the same powers he's going to use to level the city by the end of the day. He is the man responsible for the attack on our precinct. He's responsible for the death of our officers. Everything that has happened has been a part of his plot to destroy the city."

West let out a deep breath. "Let's say I believe you, Bishop, and I want to. As much as I would love to get my hands around the neck of the man responsible for hitting our precinct, how do we know this wizard was the mind behind it? How do we know that he is holed up in that apartment tower? The whole city is on edge. The last thing we need is for the police to ram-raid a private property. It would only serve to further heighten everyone's state of alarm. People could be injured or killed—not to mention my officers. There's just not enough actionable evidence to support an assault of that magnitude. Call me a skeptic, but the notion that these witches and wizards exist right under our very nose is a little difficult for me to believe."

"You say that, Chief, but I've been under your nose for months and you're still having trouble believing that witches exist and magic is real," Kasey said. "There's nothing else I can do but show you." She took a step back and raised both of her palms outstretched before her. "*Pêl Tân.*"

A ball of flame flickered to life over each of her outstretched hands. Each ball of fire whirled and turned in the air as wisps of flame flickered toward the ceiling.

West's eyes went wide. The fire reflected on his glasses.

He inched away from the blaze, pressing himself back into the leather of his chair.

The room began to heat. Sweat trickled down Vida's brow as he watched in awe.

Kasey closed her left hand and the ball of fire hovering above it wisped out of existence. Still controlling the ball of fire above her right hand, she made it dance.

West's eyes followed the ball of fire as it bounced around the room as if on an invisible string.

With a flick of her wrist, Kasey extinguished the blaze. "As you can see, Chief, I am a witch, magic is very real, and so is the threat to this city. If we don't do something now, by nightfall there will be nothing left of the New York City you know and love."

West shuffled in his chair. "Now that was a more compelling argument. You're a witch, you say? Well, I'll be damned. I've seen a lot in my time, but I never would have guessed. I always figured magic is the stuff of books and movies. To see it, in my face. It's something else."

"I can only imagine, Chief," Kasey replied. "I'd love to stand here and banter about it all day, but frankly, we just don't have the time. The man you saw murder those innocent people is right now, as we speak, putting into action a plan that will destroy the city."

"She's right, sir," Vida chimed in. "If he succeeds in detonating a device deep enough beneath the city, he'll create enough seismic activity to destroy much of New York. Whatever isn't wiped out by the earthquake will surely be destroyed by the tsunami that will inevitably follow. He must be stopped, no matter the cost."

"Do you have a plan?" West asked.

"Somewhat," Kasey answered. "To be honest, we know little of what will greet us once we breach the building. We know that we will have to split up into two forces, with one clearing toward the basement and another working their way up the building, scouring floor by floor to ensure no one is able to escape. We have two objectives. We need to both stop the weapon and kill Akihiro, the wizard responsible for the plot. If he survives or, worse yet, escapes, he will simply contrive a new plan to carry out his murderous intentions. You cannot underestimate him. He was willing to kill a high-ranking member of the magical community and assume his identity for an entire year in order to bring this plan to fruition. There is nothing he won't do, no price he will not pay to achieve his objective."

Chief West drummed his fingers on the table. "What, precisely, would you have us do?"

Kasey stepped forward and sat on the edge of West's desk. "We need police to isolate the target. Establish a perimeter three blocks in every direction. Then, we need your help tightening the noose until we can choke the life out of him."

"And your positive he's in there?" West asked.

"Absolutely. We'd also like to borrow a number of tactical vehicles to help us breach the perimeter."

West nodded. "Who, exactly, is *we*?"

"Akihiro is a wizard. He will be met in kind. My people are preparing a strike force as we speak. We'll have a division of almost fifty of our most experienced combat mages. If we can secure armored transport to assist in safely reaching the target, we will dig him out of his hole."

West stood up. "We can do a lot better than simply providing transport and a perimeter. If the city is going to be destroyed, it's all or nothing. I'll reach out to the other precincts. With the additional manpower, we can lock down Park Avenue and provide close air support. I think we should consider to attempt an airborne insertion via helicopter. With tactical teams sweeping down from the rooftop, we can pincer anyone in between."

"I like the sound of that," Bishop said.

"Chief," Kasey began, "we have every reason to believe the building has been heavily fortified. The Shinigami have both magic and munitions. Anyone you send into that building is likely to die in there."

"In there, out here. If you are right about their plan for the city, it won't matter. If we fail, we're all going to die. At least in there we'll be making a difference. Besides, we're the NYPD, Kasey. We don't back down from a fight."

Kasey rose from her chair. Things were coming together, and not a moment too soon. The clock on the rear wall of the office read 10:50 am. Time was running out. The strike teams still needed to be mustered. With the NYPD providing the transportation, the Ninth Precinct made a natural rally point.

"Chief, time is of the essence. With your permission, can we rally the strike teams here at the Precinct? The city is not a safe place for our kind right now. Gathering anywhere else will draw unwanted attention."

West was silent for a moment, then he replied, "Fifty wizards, here in the precinct...I guess there has to be a first time for everything. In the meantime, I'll make a few calls to our other station chiefs. We'll bring the combined might of the NYPD down on this Akihiro."

"I'll call Sanders." Kasey reached into her jacket for her phone "He'll have them here within the hour."

The ground shook, knocking Kasey off her feet. She fell to the ground with a thud.

The sound of the blast followed.

The office windows shattered, showering the office with shards of glass. Kasey turned away as the deadly rain descended. Her leather jacket protected her from the worst of it.

It's too early. This can't be happening now. We still have hours.

Reaching for the chair for support, Kasey pulled herself to her feet.

"What the hell was that?" West demanded bracing against the desk. "I thought you said we had time."

Kasey shook her head. "I don't know. This isn't right. This can't be happening now."

She darted to the window and, careful to avoid the shards of glass on the sill, searched the skyline. It was clear. No emerald green tinged smoke as she had expected. In her visions, it had always wafted up through the cracks in the shattered street.

Then it came. A thick plume of dust rose into the air.

Searching for the source of the blast, Kasey turned her gaze to the street below.

The dust was rising from the station below.

If it's not the attack on the city, then what?

The street was devoid of police officers, but a dozen vehicles blocked the street before the station. Men were piling out of the vans and trucks and drawing weapons. Vida appeared beside her at the window.

A cold tingle ran up Kasey's spine. It was déjà vu. She'd seen the same sight from the fourth floor of the Night Crew stash house as their reinforcements had arrived.

What are they doing here? Are they in league with Akihiro?

It made no sense. Their hit man had been left for dead and Kasey had long since ditched the money that they had been using to track her. How had the Night Crew found her?

"What is it, Kasey? What's going on?" Bishop asked, getting to her feet.

Kasey glanced over her shoulder at Bishop. "We have company and not the good kind."

"Akihiro?" West asked, reaching into his desk for his pistol.

"Nope. From the look of them, I'd say Night Crew, and their timing couldn't be worse." Kasey stepped away from the window. "Chief, you're going to need a much bigger gun."

"Why are they here?" West demanded.

Kasey glanced out the window in time to see a number of the Night Crew turn their weapons on the shattered window of West's office.

"They're likely here for me," Kasey replied. "Get down!"

She grabbed Vida and pulled him away from the window.

Gunshots rang out from the street as a deadly fusillade bracketed the window frame and office ceiling.

When the gunfire ceased, West turned to Kasey. "Why is it that everyone wants to kill you?"

"In my defense, it's not always my fault," Kasey replied, her mind racing as she thought of the Night Crew swarming on the street below.

"How about this time, Kasey?" Bishop asked pointing to the street.

Kasey nodded. "I'm not going to lie, Bishop, it's definitely a possibility. It seems I stirred up quite the hornet's nest. The Night Crew must have ID'd me from the FBI's broadcasts. I may have got off their most wanted list, but it seems like the Night Crew aren't the forgive and forget type."

As the four of them hunkered on the floor of West's office, a phone rang loudly, puncturing the momentary silence.

"It's mine," West said, reaching for the desk. Picking it up, he answered it and then put it on speaker. "This is West."

"Chief West, we have a call coming through the switchboard. It's the men outside. They want to speak to you," the voice announced.

"Put them through., West replied.

"West?" a voice on the line asked in a thick accent. Kasey couldn't quite place it, but she knew it was Eastern European.

"This is West. Who is this?"

"My name is not important. What is important, is what I want. There is a young woman in your station. She's been a tremendous inconvenience to our organization. Her name is Kasey Chase. We've come to collect her."

"You can't seriously believe I would hand one of my own over to you," West replied.

"Consider carefully, West. That blast was just the first. Consider it my warning. The Ninth Precinct can lose many lives today, or it can lose just the one. Send out the woman or we'll come in and fetch her out ourselves. If it's the latter, the blood of your officers will be on your hands."

West clenched the receiver so hard his knuckles turned white. "You want her, come and get her."

CHAPTER 6

Kasey looked at Chief West. His brow furrowed as he clenched his fist. In similar situations, most men might have traded one life for many. Particularly when that one life was someone else's life. There was no way on Earth that Chief West was ever going to make that trade. His quiet courage was one of the things that Kasey respected most about him.

Unfortunately, he was about to pay a terrible price for that courage, and Kasey just couldn't let that happen. The Ninth Precinct had suffered too many losses already.

She grabbed her phone and tossed it to Vida. "Call Sanders. Tell him the precinct is under attack. It's the Night Crew. We need reinforcements, and we need them as soon as possible."

"Kasey, where are you going?" Bishop asked.

"To deal with the Night Crew. This is our house. They have no place here. Chief, pull back your men. They are heavily outnumbered and outgunned. Have them beat a fighting retreat and direct them to fall back to the fourth floor. All we have to do is survive. Reinforcements will be here before you know it. In the meantime, I'll give them something to think about."

"You can't go out there alone," Bishop replied, almost pleading. "I'll come with you."

"I can, and I will," Kasey answered. "I need you all alive for our plan to succeed. If the Night Crew were to catch and kill any of you as retaliation for what I've done, I wouldn't be able to live with myself. Stay here, rally the precinct, and reach out to the surrounding stations. I'm going to drive these mongrels from our house."

She bolted from the room, leaving West, Bishop, and Vida huddled together in the battered office.

Every moment mattered. The floors beneath were full of officers who would resist the Night Crew. Kasey needed to put herself between them and the encroaching thugs. If she failed, at least the Night Crew would leave with what they came for, keeping the rest of the Precinct safe.

There was no way of knowing exactly how many men the Night Crew had brought, but there could be as many as a hundred of them, in and around the precinct. She needed to ensure the officers survived and fell back as they were instructed.

If I can buy us the time, I know Sanders will come through.

Kasey glanced at the elevator, but thought better of it. Any moment, the Night Crew would breach the station, and emerging from the elevator would be like stepping directly into a firing squad.

She opted for the stairs, taking them two at a time until she reached the second floor. Opening the door to the bullpen, she found the officers hunkered down, seeking cover after the explosion beneath them.

Kasey shouted at them. "The precinct is under attack. Chief West needs you to move to higher ground. Grab your weapons, lock down any perps that are here, and fall back to the fourth floor. Do not engage with the invaders unless you have no other choice. Avoid the elevator, take the stairs. I'm heading to the lobby to check for any survivors. Do not follow me, am I clear?"

The officers stared at her, their eyes wide and mouths agape.

"Now move it!" Kasey bellowed, before slamming the door. She wanted to shake them out of it and get them moving before the Night Crew stormed the bullpen.

Kasey bounded back down the stairs, headed for the first floor. Arriving at the ground floor, she cracked the door and peered into the lobby through the narrow gap.

The lobby was in ruin. Whatever weapon the Night Crew had used on the station's front door had blown it wide open. Both doors and much of the surrounding masonry had been annihilated.

Several officers lay wounded on the floor of the lobby. They had been closest to the blast. Two officers crouched down behind the lobby's information desk. The smoke was clearing, and Kasey knew that at any moment the Night Crew would enter through the breach in the station.

She raced across the lobby and dropped into a slide, coming to a stop behind the information kiosk. The officers turned, startled.

Kasey halted at the familiar face. "Easy, Morales, it's me, Chase."

"Kasey, what are you doing here? Where's Bishop?" Morales asked.

"She's up with West in his office. It's where you both need to be. Any minute now, an army of heavily armed thugs is going to come through that hole. Anyone still in this lobby is going to be cut to shreds. If you want to stay in the land of the living, I'd recommend getting out of here before they make their way inside."

"How do you know?" Morales asked.

"We saw them from West's office. They're preparing to breach, so get out of here now."

Morales glanced at the stairs. As he stood to make a run for it, half a dozen figures emerged through the smoke.

The Night Crew was on the move.

Kasey grabbed Morales and yanked him back down behind the kiosk.

"What the—"

Morales didn't get to finish his sentence, as automatic weapons fire sliced through the lobby. The assault rifles blasted chunks out of the information desk, sending splinters and shards of timber in every direction.

"We're pinned down," Morales muttered. "We'll never make the stairs now."

"They are thugs, not soldiers," Kasey replied. "They have no discipline. When they reload, hit them with everything you've got. Then, when they drop, make a break for the stairs and don't look back."

The staccato bursts from the assault rifles continued to lay waste to the lobby. If it wasn't for the shelter provided by the kiosk, neither she nor the officers would have stood a chance.

After a few short seconds, the magazines ran dry. As the firing ceased, she shouted, "Now!"

The officers reached around the edge of the kiosk and opened fire with their sidearms. Silhouetted by a light streaming through the shattered front of the station, the thugs were horribly exposed. Morales and his partner fired with grim efficiency and the thugs were cut down.

As soon as the bodies hit the ground, the two officers sprung to their feet and made their run for the stairs. Kasey stood to follow them, but the next wave of Night Crew stepped into the lobby, rifles at the shoulder, ready to fire.

Morales and his partner were caught in the open. They glanced over their shoulder as the thugs drew a bead on them, across the open lobby. It was a killing ground.

"*Mellt!*" Kasey bellowed.

There was a deafening peal of thunder that echoed through the room as lightning leapt from Kasey's outstretched hands. The lightning bolt struck the first of the thugs, before arcing through the group. They were thrown back across the lobby.

The bodies struck the ground, where they twitched briefly before going still. The Night Crew were here to kill her; she wasn't going to hold any punches.

She turned to see Morales and his partner standing there, staring at her slack jawed.

"What part of get out of here don't you understand?" she snapped. "I'll hold them off for as long as I can. Get as many people as you can to the safety of the fourth floor. We need to concentrate our forces."

Morales grabbed his partner and shoved him toward the stairs. He threw Kasey an appreciative nod before he disappeared into the staircase.

The arcane assault seemed to have given the Night Crew pause. Kasey hunkered down, leaning on the kiosk to conceal most of her profile, while still keeping sight of the entrance. She had no doubt the Night Crew would come again. If anything, she'd confirmed her presence in the station.

A megaphone crackled to life. "There you are, Kasey. I thought you were in there. It seems your companions are unwilling to give you up, but I'll make you the same offer I made them. Hand yourself over to us, and we will leave. No one else needs to die today. Give your fellow officers their lives back."

Kasey sighed. The dust was clearing, and she could make out the shapes moving beyond it. Any moment now, they would come barreling back through it in force.

I just need to buy time.

Kasey raised her right hand and whispered, *"Pêl Tân."*

With all her focus, she hurled the fireball through the open portal into the street. She couldn't see what she had hit, but from the surprised screams, she knew that at least one Night Crewman had been caught in the inferno.

"Come on in," Kasey shouted. "I can do this all day long."

A devastating fusillade came pouring in through the breach. Kasey hit the deck, as round after round was pumped into the information kiosk. The Night Crew had no hesitation. Whoever was driving the assault was more than willing to sacrifice his men to take her.

Not for the first time, Kasey wondered if she and Sanders hadn't made a horrible mistake in provoking the Night Lord. It seemed there was no length he wouldn't go to avenge the losses he'd suffered. He seemed indifferent to the lives lost, but his drugs and his money, those had hit a nerve. It seemed Kasey and Sanders had done damage to his operation. Damage that he would see repaid in blood.

There was a dull thud as something struck the tile floor and skittered across it. The item came to a halt as it hit the kiosk. Kasey couldn't see it, but her gut told her to move. Summoning her protective shield, she made a break for the stairs.

Two seconds later, it detonated. The grenade blasted apart the kiosk, sending a hail of deadly shrapnel in every direction. Kasey felt the impacts as the deadly shards of steel sliced at her protective ward. Glancing over her shoulder, she saw the Night Crew streaming in through the entryway.

This time it wasn't a handful of thugs—it was an army. Dozens of them took up firing positions.

Kasey slipped into the stairway before the thugs had time to realize where she had gone.

"She must be in here somewhere. Spread out and find her," a voice demanded.

Kasey peered around the corner and caught her first glimpse of the man that was hunting her. He stood in the midst of the Night Crew, barking orders. His men raced to carry out his directives.

The man was squat, perhaps only five and a half feet tall. His hair was clipped close to his scalp except for where a scar ran from above his left eye, back into his hairline. He was wearing a bullet-proof vest, and he carried a pistol in one hand and a megaphone in the other.

The Night Crew were making swift progress. New York City might have been in disarray, but they were still attacking a police station in broad daylight. It wouldn't be long before reinforcements arrived from neighboring precincts.

With the Night Crew clustered close together, Kasey took advantage of the opportunity. *"Cerrig Wedi Torri"*.

As she barked the words of power, all eyes turned to the stairwell. Kasey's spell slammed into the tiles in front of them. The arcane energy blasted them apart like a supernatural frag grenade. The force of the explosion rolled outward, shattering tile and Night Crewmen alike.

Scarface grabbed the Night Crewman standing beside him and yanked him to the front. Kasey watched in wide-eyed amazement as the shrapnel cut the helpless meat shield to shreds.

As the energy dissipated, Scarface tossed aside his used subordinate and raised his pistol. Kasey retreated as three shots slammed into the inner wall of the precinct's internal staircase.

"After her!" Scarface shouted. When no one moved, he bellowed again, "What are you waiting for? Get her now, or it will be all of our heads."

"Didn't you see that?" a Night Crewman responded. "What the hell are we meant to do about that? She'll kill us as soon as we step into the staircase."

A gunshot rang out, followed by the distinct sound of a body dropping to the floor.

Scarface's voice threatened. "And *I'll* kill you if you don't. One of those is a possibility, the others is a certainty. Now get up those stairs before I put a bullet in the rest of you."

Kasey raced up the stairs as quick as her legs would take her. Sweat ran down her face. The Night Crew were wasting precious time and requiring her to expend much of the energy she would need to face Akihiro.

She had thinned their numbers, but in her heart, she knew it wasn't enough. There was still too many of them. She reached the second-floor landing, before the Night Crew had even hit the first step.

The sound of them stomping up the stairs beneath her caused her heart to race, but she simply kept running.

Reaching the third floor, she paused and planned her ambush, hoping the Night Crew would grow complacent in their chase. The sound of the bullpen being ransacked rose from below. She prayed that none of her colleagues were still inside.

Other Night Crew still pressed on, heading up the stairs toward her.

As the first of them rounded the corner and came into sight, Kasey unleashed hell. *"Dwrn O Aer!"*

The concussive wave rolled down the narrow staircase. It struck the lead thug, and he collected two of his companions as he hurtled back into the wall. His head struck the concrete with a sickening thud before he dropped to the landing. Whether he was dead or unconscious, Kasey didn't know, and she had no intention of hanging around to find out.

She dashed up the last of the stairs and burst onto the fourth floor only to find found dozens of weapons pointed at her.

"Easy, boys, that's Kasey," Bishop warned from behind an upturned desk. "Hold your fire."

The fourth floor had been turned into a makeshift fortress. The desks had been flipped over and were facing the stairs and the elevator. Officers were huddled down in every nook and cranny, taking cover behind chairs and tables with their weapons drawn, ready to sell their lives.

"They're right behind me," Kasey said, panting. "Shoot first and ask questions later. Their leader just executed one of his own men in cold blood. That's the measure of their resolve. They won't hesitate to kill any one of us."

"Then move your ass and take cover," Bishop called, her weapon trained firmly on the staircase.

Kasey raced across the room and hunkered beside Bishop.

"Mind if I share your desk?" Kasey asked.

"By all means," Bishop answered. "There's no one I'd rather have watching my back."

Kasey took a deep breath to calm her racing heart. As she let it out, the first of the Night Crew appeared at the top of the stairs.

The officers of the Ninth Precinct opened fire. Framed by the open door, it was almost impossible to miss the thugs. Three of the Night Crew fell, riddled with bullets.

"Hold your fire," West shouted.

The firing ceased.

"There are still plenty more of them to come. We need to conserve our ammunition. Pick your targets and shoot to kill."

"Chief, look, the elevator," an officer shouted.

Kasey turned as the floor readout on two of the elevators flashed. They began at the ground floor and were rising.

2nd Floor, 3rd Floor.

The elevators crawled upward. Every eye on the room was fixed on them. So intent were they on watching the approaching elevators that Kasey almost missed the arm that reached around the doorway and hurled an object into the densely packed office.

Her heart stopped as her eyes locked on the MKII fragmentation grenade, bouncing across the floor toward her.

There was nowhere left to run.

CHAPTER 7

Time came to a standstill as Kasey stared at the grenade. If it detonated, it would kill everyone in the room.

She couldn't let that happen. Standing up, she drew deep on her arcane energy. She was exhausted, but if her gambit didn't work her fatigue would be the least of her worries.

She mouthed the words for a protective ward while in her heart she sent up a silent prayer that it would be enough. With a deep breath, she stepped around the desk and, before giving it another thought, leapt onto the grenade.

"Kasey, no!" Bishop shouted.

As Kasey hit the floor, she heard the click as the grenade detonated.

The blast threw her clear across the room, slamming her into the wall. She slumped to the floor in a heap.

Her head was ringing. She felt like she'd been run over by a truck, only to have it stop and reverse back over her. She tried to move but her body wouldn't respond. The elevator chimed, and out of the corner of her eye she saw the aluminum doors part.

The assembled officers opened fire. Clearly, the Night Crew had expected less resistance after the grenade. The men in the elevator found themselves staring at their own personal firing squad.

The Night Crew barely got a shot off before they were gunned down.

Silence fell over the room.

West strode to the elevator. "Luiz, Simmons, check the bodies, make sure they're down for the count. Take the weapons and their ammunition. There are still plenty more of them below. We'll need every weapon we can get our hands on."

Luiz and Simmons, ran over to assist West. The officers began relieving the fallen thugs of their weapons: AR15 assault rifles, with spare magazines. They would come in useful.

"Chief, what do you want me to do with these?" one of the officers said, holding up a pair of grenades.

"I'll take those," Chief West replied, lifting them out of the officer's hands.

With practiced ease, Chief West pulled the pins out of the grenades and lobbed them through the open doorway into the stairwell.

"Grenade!" shouted a member of the Night Crew from below, followed by the flurry of footsteps.

The frag grenades exploded, shaking the building as they turned the staircase into a killing ground.

"That ought to buy us some reprieve," West said, "Bishop, see to Kasey. The rest of you, we won't get that lucky a second time. Morales, take one of the rifles and watch the stairs. If they get back onto the landing, we'll have more grenades to contend with. If anyone pokes their head up, take it off. Simmons, jam the elevators so they can't make another trip."

Footsteps scurried toward Kasey, and then Bishop was crouching beside her.

She could feel Bishop's hands as she examined her, looking for wounds. Slowly, Kasey wriggled her fingers to test their motion.

"I swear, Kasey, one of these days you are going to get yourself killed," Bishop muttered.

Kasey spluttered as she tried to catch a breath. "Not today." Grabbing Bishop's hands, she squeezed them. "It's okay, Bishop. I'm fine. The shield took the worst of the brunt."

Bishop threw her arms around Kasey. "You're insane, you know that. Never do anything like that again."

"If I didn't, you'd all be dead. I'd do it again in a heartbeat," Kasey replied. "But on the brighter side, I guess it would have spared me a lecture."

Bishop gave Kasey a light-hearted shove, as Chief West crouched down beside her. "Easy, Bishop, that's no way to say thank you. That was a brave move, Chase. I'm glad you're okay. Any ideas as to what we should do next? You've faced these guys before. How did you beat them last time?"

Kasey pulled herself up against the wall, leaning on it to steady herself. "To be honest, Sanders and I didn't beat them. We hit their safe house, stole their cash, and torched their product. We fought our way free as their reinforcements showed up. We figured we'd overstayed our welcome. If we want to beat this lot, we're going to have to kill them all or hold them off for long enough that they realize their mission has become untenable. The longer we hold them off, the more time we give our reinforcements to arrive. We just have to give Sanders and the other precincts a chance."

"Easier said than done," West replied. "In spite of their losses, it seems like they are already massing again. We can't hold them off forever. Eventually, they'll break through or manage to get another grenade in here and then we are toast."

Footsteps echoed up the stairwell. There were still dozens of Night Crew willing to press the issue.

Scarface's megaphone crackled to life. "You know, Miss Chase, while the Night Lord may have wanted you alive, I'm sure he'll settle for your corpse. If we can't drag you out of the precinct, we'll bring it down with you all inside it. You seem to have fortified your position but a fat lot of good that's going to do when we blast the floor out from beneath you. You have until my men arrive with the blasting charges to surrender yourself to save your comrades. Otherwise, you'll die up there together. Your choice, Miss Chase. Don't take long. They'll be back any minute."

Kasey reached out her hand. "Help me up."

Bishop and West took an arm each and hoisted Kasey to her feet. She limped over to the shattered window.

"What are you looking for, Kasey?" Bishop asked, following behind her.

"He mentioned that his men had to fetch the breaching charges. Look down there. There they are." Kasey pointed to where two men were lifting a black case out of the back of a van.

"We need to take them down. If those charges reach the third floor, they're going to blow the floor out from beneath us and drag my body back to the Night Lord as a trophy."

"What are you suggesting?" Bishop asked.

Kasey searched the street. "Bring the rifles. We need to stop them making it back into the station."

West beckoned to Luiz, who raced over to the window. Resting the AR15 against the window ledge, he laid down a withering hail of suppressing fire. The Night Crew dropped the crate and bolted behind the nearby van. With the explosives' progress halted at least for the moment, Kasey breathed a sigh of relief.

As the Night Crew on the street below raised their weapons, Kasey and her companions hit the deck.

"You can't let them get that case into the building," West shouted.

Kasey stretched up just enough to glance over the edge of the window. A Night Crewman was racing towards the case.

"One of them is making a run for it," she said.

Luiz stood up and let off a three-round burst. The second shot found its mark and the Night Crewman went down, only a few short steps from his goal.

The thugs below returned fire. Luiz gasped, stumbling backwards. He dropped his rifle as he fell, blood pooling on his uniform from the gunshot wound in his right shoulder.

"We need something to staunch the bleeding," Kasey said. "Don't worry, Luiz, you'll be fine."

Luiz grimaced.

"There are some hand towels in my bathroom. Bishop, can you grab them?" West asked.

Bishop raced for the bathroom to fetch the towels.

"Check on the case," Kasey said, handing Luiz's rifle to West. "If they get it into the building, we'll be able to measure our life expectancy with an egg timer."

West glanced out the window. "Oh, what now? Who the hell are these fools?"

"What fools?" Kasey asked. "The Night Crew?

"I don't think so," West replied. "Just rounded the corner, strolling down the street like they own the place."

Bishop appeared, towels in hand.

Kasey pressed Bishop's hand, still gripping the towel, to Luiz's wound. "Help Luiz hold this, please. I need to take a look."

She stood up and spotted them immediately.

Twenty people strolled down East 5th Street. West was right, they advanced without a care in the world. Most of them were dressed from head to toe in black fatigues, balaclavas, and bullet proof vests. Many of them were packing submachine guns. More concerning perhaps were those who were seemingly unarmed.

Only two of them were not wearing masks. The first was a tall olive-skinned man whose black hair almost reached his open-necked black dress shirt. Gold suspenders held up his black slacks. The holsters slung under his arms were empty, the pistols already in his hands.

Hades.

At his side sashayed his girlfriend, Zryx. She wore tight leather pants and a tank top. Her short hair was styled into sharply pointed spikes. Her mouth was twisted into a grin that wasn't the least bit comforting. It was a face Kasey had hoped never to see again.

"Kasey, do you know these guys? Are they friends of yours?" West asked.

Kasey scratched her neck. "Yes, I do, but I don't know where we stand. The last time I saw her, she pulled a gun on me. We didn't exactly part on good terms."

"Who are they?" West asked.

Kasey pointed at the street. "The one with the pistols is Hades."

"Hades, like the Greek god?" West asked.

"Yes. He's not from your world—he's from mine. He runs New York's criminal underworld."

West shook his head. "I've never heard of him."

"Consider that a blessing," Kasey replied. "The night I met him, he tossed me into a cage to fight for my life."

"So not a friend?" West asked.

Hades answered the question for him. Without breaking his stride, he opened fire onto the Night Crew. His men added their fire to the fray.

The Night Crew, already occupied with the police before them, were caught flat-footed by the appearance of Hades and his men. The ambush quickly became a bloodbath. The Night Crew scrambled for cover behind their vehicles but there was no reprieve.

Hades' unarmed companions lashed out. The first hurled a fireball into a sedan. It took only moments before the conflagration superheated the vehicle and detonated its gas tank. The blast took out both Night Crewmen who were huddled behind it.

A wizard to Hades' left hurled a blast of energy into one of the Night Crew's van. The blast of energy flipped the van, crushing another assailant.

Without mercy, Hades and his entourage carved a path through the Night Crew arrayed before the Precinct. With a flick of his wrist, one of the wizards hauled a Night Crewman into the air. Hades executed the hovering thug with a single shot.

As the body dropped, Hades locked eyes with Kasey. Closing her mouth, Kasey blinked at the clinical display before her. Hades raised his right pistol to his brow in a mock salute, before dropping another thug with the pistol in his left.

In moments, the street was clear of Night Crewmen. Hades' cohorts dropped their spent magazines and reloaded before entering the station.

Gunfire rang out from the floor beneath as the Night Crew found themselves in the unenviable position of being caught between Hades below and the police above.

Footsteps in the stairwell signaled the Night Crew's renewed assault. A last-ditch effort to achieve their goal. Shielded by the door jam, Morales opened fire. The Night Crew's disjointed assault carried them straight into the waiting guns of the Ninth Precinct.

When Morales ceased firing, Kasey glanced down the stairwell. More than a dozen bodies lined its interior. None were moving. Morales reloaded a fresh magazine, but the station had gone quiet.

Kasey was about to venture out onto the landing when a singsong tone carried up the stairwell. "Jenny, my old friend, is that you?"

It was Hades. He was using the alibi from the night they had first met. Kasey was under no misapprehensions; Hades knew exactly who she was.

"Jenny, do tell your friends to lower their weapons," he continued. "Your thuggish friends are dead or dying. They won't be needing them, and my Helldrakes and I would hate for any miscommunication to result in unnecessary bloodletting."

"Jenny? Who the hell is Jenny?" West asked.

"It's me," Kasey whispered. "It's the alias I was using when I was on the run. It's okay, Chief, lower your weapons. You saw them at work. If they were here to kill us, there isn't a lot we could do about it anyway. We are low on ammunition and I'm exhausted. I couldn't take the lot of them, even if I wanted to. We're better off talking it through and finding out what they are here for."

West nodded, but his furrowed brow conveyed his skepticism. He turned to his officers. "It's all right, men, lower your weapons."

The officers of the Ninth Precinct holstered their pistols and laid down their rifles.

Kasey called down the stairwell. "Okay, Hades," Kasey shouted. "We've lowered our weapons. Come on up."

There was a momentary silence from the floor beneath.

"Call me a skeptic, Jenny, but I'd really rather you came to us. Bring your friends if you like. We'll wait for you down here."

Kasey looked at Bishop. "What do you think?"

Bishop shrugged. "I don't know these guys, so I don't know what to think. Luiz needs a medic though. The sooner we can get him help, the better.

"Yeah, you are right," Kasey replied. "Besides, we can't stay up here all day. If we do, Akihiro wins."

Bishop rested a hand on her holster. "If we die, he also wins. What's the chance these guys are with him?"

"I doubt it. Hades thinks far too highly of himself and his little empire to let a maniac burn it down." Kasey entered the stairwell and leaned over the balustrade. "Hades, before I come down, I just wanted to check, you are aware of the recent changes at the Council, are you not?"

"Of course," he bellowed. "Out with the old, in with the new, I always say. I understand your *dear husband* has been appointed interim Chancellor. I suppose congratulations are in order." Hades' emphasis told her he knew exactly who Sanders was. He'd likely surmised it when Sanders had threatened him in the underworld.

"Husband?" Bishop asked, her jaw dropping. "You have been busy."

"It was an alias. Things didn't get that crazy. Don't worry, you didn't miss the ceremony." Kasey replied, giving her a small shove. "Okay, Hades, we're coming down. Keep in mind, if anything does happen to me, you'll have earned the undying attention of the Council's current chancellor. He'll be most displeased if anything was to happen to his wife."

"Of course, Jenny. Who do you think it was that sent us?"

Kasey let out a sigh of relief. "Alright, Hades, we're coming down."

She made her way down the stairwell with West and Bishop right behind her.

The grenades West had lobbed down the stairs had found their mark. Five Night Crew had been caught in the blast and had died horribly. Others had retreated into the room, likely taking cover from Hades and his men.

The third floor of the Ninth Precinct was an open plan office, with lengthy workbenches running in rows down the room. On a normal day, officers would have been manning the stations and working on case files. Today, it was a charnel house.

More than a dozen Night Crew lay draped over benches or dead on the floor. There wasn't a single Night Crew man still moving. Hades and his men had been swift, efficient, and deadly.

Inside the battered office, they found Hades changing the magazine on his pistol. His pet was at his side, knife in hand, cleaning her nails.

Kasey was loath to go anywhere near her. Not because she was afraid of the knife. In Kasey's estimation, Hades' pet was unhinged. There was no telling what she might do or why. Even Hades' presence seemed little guarantee she would behave herself.

Hades' other men were scattered throughout the room. It took Kasey a moment to realize they were relieving the Night Crew of their weapons and were stacking the guns in a pile in the center of the room.

"Oh, Jenny. I've missed you," Hades began. His pet snarled, but didn't look up. "Shall I call you Jenny, or can we dispense with that charade now that it has served its purpose?"

Kasey approached him. "I'm not gonna lie, Hades, I was hoping to never see you again."

Hades places hand on his chest. "You wound me, Miss Chase. After all, I'm one of your biggest fans. Dozer is still recovering from that walloping you gave him, but I digress. Is that any way to talk to someone who just saved your life?"

Kasey bit her lip. "You're right, Hades. I'm glad you showed up when you did. Things were starting to get a little rocky. How did you know we were in trouble?"

"Sanders called us earlier, looking for help with your genocidal wizard. When I asked to speak with you, he told me you were out rallying reinforcements. When I heard the Night Crew were on the move, we put two and two together. Between you and me, paying us with cash you stole from the Night Crew should have earned you both a death sentence, but let's face it, the two of you are so damn crazy, I love it. You have balls the size of Brooklyn. Figuratively speaking."

It had been brazen, to be sure. After Kasey had been confronted by the Night Crew assassin, she had been worried about what might have blown back on Hades. She had no way of knowing how he would react to being dragged into the feud.

Being hunted by the Night Crew was one thing; being hunted by Hades as well would have taken her problems to a whole new level.

"May I ask, what you are planning to do with the weapons?" West asked, pointing to the mounting pile of munitions in the center of the room.

"Spoils of war," Hades replied. "We don't work for free, you know."

West shook his head, "You can't just take those. They're evidence."

"We can, and we are, officer. Their previous owners no longer require them, and frankly, you are in no position to stop us. In fact, you'd be better off pretending you never saw us at all." Hades smiled as he gestured emphatically with his pistol.

Kasey squirmed. West would not take well to being threatened.

"Are you threatening me?" West asked, his cheeks flushing. "Do that again and you'll spend the rest of your life in a cell."

Hades smile disappeared and his eyes narrowed on West. "Don't push your luck, Chief. Circumstances may have put us on the same side today, but if you ever try to make good on that threat, you'll be as dead as these fools here. My Helldrakes will see to that, understand?"

West ground his teeth so hard it was audible. If he had more to say, he was holding it in.

"Good." Hades gave a cold smile. "I'm glad to see we have an understanding. Boys, take the guns and toss them in the cars. Miss Chase and I have a lot to discuss."

The Helldrakes scooped up armloads of rifles and proceeded to carry them straight out the door and down the stairs, past the watchful eyes of the Ninth Precinct.

Kasey looked around the room, at the Night Crew bodies scattered everywhere. Her gaze darted from body to body.

"What are you looking for?" Hades asked. "They're not getting back up, I can promise you that."

"It's not that," Kasey replied, turning to look at the bodies in the stairwell. "On your way through, did you see a short one with a scar over his left eye? He should have been carrying a megaphone. He was their leader."

Hades shook his head. "Can't say that I did. I'll be honest, though, I wasn't exactly paying close attention. If it moved, we shot it. If it didn't stop, we shot it again. The one with the scar, he a friend of yours?"

Exhaustion overtook her. Everything was getting to be too much. She leaned on the edge of a desk as she drew in a breath and let it out. "Not really, but I would have liked to have a chat with him about his boss. Their love for me and Sanders is starting to get in the way of us saving the city. They'll die with the rest of us when Akihiro detonates his weapon. They need to understand that."

"The Night Lord is not a forgiving foe, Kasey. When this business with the Shinigami is done, you are going to have your work cut out dealing with him," Hades warned.

"A problem for another day," Kasey replied, straightening. She folded her arms. "I take it Sanders told you what we are up against."

Hades slipped his pistols back into their holsters. "Yes. I didn't leave him much choice. After Akihiro butchered a dozen of my Helldrakes on prime-time TV, I demanded answers. Outing our community like that may have bought Akihiro some breathing room, but it's also forced our hands. While we may see the world very differently, Miss Chase, rest assured, we still want it to continue, and no ancient death cult is going to take it from us. Before the day is through, I'll see him suffer for what he has done."

"You'll have to get in line," West answered. "There are more than a few of us with an axe to grind with these Shinigami. They killed more than twenty of my men."

Hades turned to the chief. "My apologies, with all the excitement earlier, we haven't been properly introduced, Chief...?"

"West. Chief West," West replied.

Hades placed a hand on his chest. "Of course, I forget my manners. Chief West, it's a genuine pleasure. I'm Hades, Lord of the Underworld, delighted to make your acquaintance."

He stretched out his palm.

West took it, his steel gray eyes studying Hades intently.

"Come now, Chief, you may not know me, you may not like me—in fact, that look in your eye says I make your skin crawl—but why not belay that thought. The enemy of my enemy is my friend. So today, that makes us friends. Let us set our differences aside while we destroy the Shinigami. What say you?"

West nodded. "What about tomorrow?"

"If there *is* a tomorrow," Kasey replied forcing the two men's hands apart. "We'll cross that bridge when we come to it. In the meantime, you all play nice, while I track down Sanders and his agents. We'll have them rally here, lay the final plans for the assault, and be on our way. Chief, can you get the other precincts moving? We're going to need a clear run to Park Avenue, and any transportation you can get us."

"I'll get it done," West replied, heading for the stairs.

Kasey turned to face the room. "Bishop and Vida, can you see to the wounded?"

"What are you going to do?" Bishop asked, coming up beside her.

"Once Sanders is on his way, I'm going to steal as much rest as I can get, and then Akihiro is going to rue the day he decided to set foot in my city."

CHAPTER 8

The ground floor of the Ninth Precinct station had been obliterated. Broken glass and shattered concrete were strewn across the length of the once pristine lobby. The information desk that Kasey had taken shelter behind was no longer in existence. Its broken remnants lay scattered to the four corners of the room. Bullet holes pockmarked the wall, the floors, and even the ceiling. The steel doors of the station along with ten feet of concrete wall had been demolished.

Inside the devastated lobby, the bodies had been removed, but the blood and ruin remained. There was no time for cleaning.

What had been a battleground only an hour earlier now hosted one of the most unusual meetings in modern times. It had been centuries since wizards and normals stood shoulder to shoulder in a common cause. The dark ages had seen to that. Witch Hunts and Inquisitions had swept Europe, forcing the World of Magic underground and turning magic into a myth for the ages. Five centuries of skepticism and prejudice had divided these worlds. Now, a common foe had brought them together: Akihiro Igarashi, Master of the Shinigami and the man holding New York City and the lives of everyone in it, in his grasp.

Survival is a powerful motivator.

Kasey looked over the assembled parties. Hades and his Helldrakes stood at the ready. Eighteen ruthless assassins, clad head to toe in black cloth and Kevlar that both concealed their identity and provided state of the art protection from weapons fire. While his men stood in silence, Hades' gaze darted about, alternating between scanning the room's entrances and exits and studying the other parties clustered about him, specifically the growing police presence.

Kasey got the impression that he didn't spend a whole lot of time above ground. Being out in the open and surrounded by so much law enforcement was clearly not his idea of a good day out. Hades' discomfort only multiplied when Sanders arrived at the head of a contingent of ADI agents. The ADI had deployed as many agents as it could muster. More than fifty wizards stood shoulder to shoulder with their new chancellor. Wearing bullet-proof vests over their dress shirts and slacks, it was an odd sight, but Kasey couldn't help but stare in awe at the potent display of arcane power they represented.

The Ninth Precinct had gathered what remained of its strength. Many of its wounded officers had been dispatched to local hospitals, but those that were still standing were as resolute as ever. The Fighting Ninth never backed down from a fight. In the battle for New York City, they would give it everything they had. Bishop, Morales, and Henley stood alongside a dozen of their colleagues, hovering uneasily between the groups of wizards. Kasey was relieved to see Henley had survived the station's siege. He had been on patrol when the station had been hit by the Night Crew.

The Ninth Precinct was ready for war. Twice now, war had found its way into the Fighting Ninth's home, and there was no way in hell they were going to take it lying down. The opportunity to settle the score with the Shinigami was one they would not let pass.

West excused himself to coordinate with the adjoining precincts. Closing down and evacuating three city blocks was no simple exercise. It would require the deployment of NYPD resources on a grand scale. Trying to vacate and evacuate part of the city in broad daylight without alerting the Shinigami to their intention was an almost impossible task. Nonetheless, West had set about it with every shred of cunning and resource at his disposal. Local units had already begun a gradual evacuation of the buildings at the periphery of the strike zone. As the assault commenced, the evacuation would escalate as the police cordon tightened to ensure Akihiro could not escape or endanger the lives of other innocent bystanders.

So, it comes down to this. Less than 100 souls. I hope it's enough. It has to be enough.

"Bishop, Morales, Hades, Sanders, let's bring it in." Kasey began. "We're running out of time. We need to get moving before they detonate the weapon."

The heads of the respective strike forces gathered around a planning table while their divisions looked on patiently. Hades' pet made as if to follow him, but he raised his hand to stop her. A flush of red flashed across her face. As Kasey locked eyes with her, Hades' pet snarled.

Kasey shrugged off the hostility. She had no time for such nonsense now.

As the leader of each element gathered closer, Kasey addressed them. "Alright, everyone, I know we've had our differences in the past, but I'm glad that everyone here is willing to set them aside for the good of the city and the lives of everyone who remains in it. You have all heard what we are up against. Many of you have seen it firsthand. Understand in no uncertain terms, if Akihiro's plot is not stopped, the entire city will be destroyed, along with everyone in it. There is no bargaining or reasoning with him. He has spent years working to bring this to fruition. If he succeeds, he will both devastate this country and gather the life force of millions of its citizens. Akihiro believes this will grant him immortality."

"Will it?" Bishop asked. "Is that even possible?"

Sanders tapped his hand on the table. "We've seen him use another's life force to heal himself, but to be honest, we don't know what harvesting life force on that scale will accomplish. The study of necromancy is forbidden, both here and the rest of the civilized world. Taking a life to harness its energy for oneself is a crime that cannot be countenanced and is not tolerated in any form.

"The Shinigami give no heed to our laws. They have existed in secret for centuries. The council had sought to root them out, with no success. They hide underground in countries where our influence holds no sway. This is the first time they have been on US soil in a century. We need to end them here, now, before he can detonate the device."

"We're on a clock people," Kasey replied. "If we haven't successfully disarmed the device by five pm, everything will be lost. The city and everyone in it will perish."

Hades glanced at his Rolex. "It's almost two pm now. That doesn't give us a whole lot of time."

"You're right. We're almost out of time, which is why this is so crucial. Every one of us needs to play our part, if we are to have a chance at stopping him," Kasey said, brushing her hair back behind her ear.

"What do we know about the target?" Bishop asked. "What are we walking into?"

Sanders leaned on the desk. Pointing at the map of Manhattan, he said, "My men have been watching 432 Park Avenue for weeks. We know that Akihiro has a number of acolytes at his disposal. After the incidents here and at the council, it's safe to say they are heavily armed. We also believe he has numerous wizards who have defected to his cause. We'll face both magical and mundane firepower as we attempt to breach the building.

"Park Avenue itself has been heavily fortified. While it's still under construction, most of the building is hidden behind temporary fencing. We haven't been able to get inside, but our agents have scouted it from the adjacent properties. He has been busy barricading his position. Several anti-vehicle impediments have been constructed inside the barrier. To the untrained eyes, they appear to be construction materials, but we know better. The panoramic windows that have been already installed on the lower floors have been blacked out or covered. We've been unable to get a good look inside the building, but it's safe to say that whatever is waiting for us in there will be equally hostile," Sanders concluded.

"What about the adjacent buildings?" Hades asked.

"The adjacent buildings?" Kasey asked. "The police will clear them. Why?"

"Your target is surrounded on every side by vantage points with clear lines of fire. It's a sniper's dream. If we're caught in the open, we'll be cut down. Those buildings pose as much of a threat as the target itself."

"You're right," Kasey replied. "We'll be using armored carriers for the insertion. The police are going to ensure we have a clear route to the target. We'll be borrowing armored personnel carriers belonging to the various precincts of the city. Chief West has requisitioned their use. They should allow us swift and safe passage through the city and allow us to make an armored insertion into the ground floor of the Park Avenue complex. They will withstand any small arms fire until we reach our destination. We will clear the ground floor and lock it down. Once inside, we'll be safe from any external over watch they have positioned. The same black out windows will protect us once we are inside. We'll leave a contingent led by the Helldrakes and the Ninth Precinct to ensure that no one can enter or exit the building. A joint strike force of officers will accompany Sanders and me as we breach the subbasement and make our way down into the building. Vida, what do you think we can expect to find?"

Vida laid a set of blueprints on the table and rolled them out. "These are the original construction plans filed with city council. Be aware that 432 Park Avenue is the tallest residential building in the western hemisphere. Its foundations are equally as impressive, descending deep within the earth. On their own, they took a year to construct. It is our belief that somewhere beneath the building, within those foundations, they have prepared means to drill further. I believe that somewhere in the subbasement of the building we are going to find some sort of tunneling or boring machine. That boring machine will be tunneling deeper, and it is probably designed to detonate an explosive weapon deep beneath the city. It's likely they have been tunneling for some time. Sanders and Kasey's contingent will need to be prepared. They will need to clear swiftly through the subbasement. They will need to find that weapon and disarm it before it can reach detonation depth. To that end, officers from our bomb squad here at the Ninth Precinct will accompany them. Once the weapon has been taken out of commission, you can return to the surface and sweep the building floor by floor. Akihiro will be cornered." Vida looked around the table. "Remember, this man is armed and extremely dangerous. You can't give him any quarter."

"Exactly," Kasey replied. "At the same time as we breach the ground floor, we will have an aerial-based insertion attack from above. Several airborne tactical units will land on top of the building and sweep down through it. Hopefully this will pressure Akihiro into the waiting guns of the Helldrakes and the Ninth Precinct who will be waiting for him. Are there any questions?"

"Just one," Hades replied. "You said wizards were defecting to his cause? Any idea how many?"

Sanders shook his head. "We have seen as many as ten enter the building and not exit. The true number could be much higher, but the reality is, they are cowards who would abandon our cause for the honeyed whisperings of a madman. They are to be shown no mercy. It doesn't matter who we face in there—when you get inside, don't hesitate. They'll not think twice about killing any one of us. We need to possess the same resolve."

"So the Arcane Council isn't going to have an issue with us killing a dozen of its citizens?" Hades asked.

"If they are not with us, they are against us," Sanders said. "The ADI and Arcane Council have no tolerance for those who would carry out or aid in genocide to fulfill their own selfish ambitions. Make no mistake, Akihiro is committed. We have no idea how long he's been planning this, but we do know he has been masquerading as Arthur Ainsley for over a year. There is no price he will not pay, no lie he will not tell. No life he will not take. If any of you succumb to his influence, we'll put you down right alongside him. Am I understood?"

"Crystal," Hades replied.

Kasey looked at the faces gathered around the table. Their steely eyed resolve echoed what was in her own heart.

Bishop gathered up the blueprints. "If there is nothing else folks, let's move out. The carriers are waiting for us out front. Let's get loaded up and get it done. Good luck and Godspeed."

CHAPTER 9

Kasey stared out through the ballistic glass of the armored vehicle, a Lenco Bearcat, as it rolled down Madison Avenue. The Bearcat was closer to a tank than a truck. Covered in military spec steel armored bodywork, and blast-resistant floor, doors, and hatches, it could easily withstand heavy gunfire while delivering a fifteen strong tactical team right into the heart of a hostile environment—a role that made it eminently suitable for its current mission.

West had done his job well. The convoy had faced little traffic as it had wound its way through the city. By the time the strike force reached Madison Avenue, the streets were deserted.

As the strike force had set out from the Ninth Precinct, Manhattan's outlying police precincts had begun an evacuation of the island. If the strike force failed, the loss of life would be immense. The NYPD would do their best to clear as many innocent civilians as it could, though Kasey knew they didn't have anywhere near the time required. Any warning Akihiro gained from the evacuation now was unlikely to do him much good. It had taken the convoy only minutes to reach their destination.

Kasey's earpiece crackled to life. "Strike force, this is Sanders. ETA sixty seconds and counting. When we engage, stay off comms unless absolutely necessary. With the size of our contingent, it will be all too easy for any radio chatter to drown out crucial communications. Ready yourselves. We're weapons hot. See you on the other side."

Every member of the strike force had been fitted with an ADI earpiece. The all-in-one communicator would allow them seamless communication within a several mile radius. Unlike standard communications equipment on the market, these earpieces were designed to work even in the underground metropolis of the Arcane Council, a quality that would be crucial in whatever labyrinthine catacombs existed beneath 432 Park Avenue.

"Roger that, Sanders," Kasey replied. "Everything is looking good here. Nothing out of the ordinary. It looks like we may have caught them napping. Let's lock and load. People, this is it."

Kasey glanced sideways at Henley who was driving the armored truck. Both hands gripped the wheel firmly. At a little over fourteen tons, the Bearcat was a mobile battering ram. Approaching the intersection of Madison Avenue and East 56th Street, he eased off the gas, but barely touched the brakes. Wrenching the wheel to the right, he brought the armored vehicle around the tight corner.

On both sides of East 56th Street, skyscrapers towered above them. They barreled past the First Republic Bank, with its terraced office building.

432 Park Avenue rose into the sky like a concrete and steel finger. Although still under construction, it towered far above its neighbors. A crane sat seemingly appended to the structure. It was a shame that the building might never be completed. Akihiro's perversion of Arthur Ainsley's dream had fitted it for a different destiny.

At the base of the structure, a temporary fence stretched away from the building's facade, obscuring the sidewalk immediately in front of the skyscraper. It ran from the First Republic Bank on the left, clear past 432 Park Avenue to a five-story glass tower resting in the shadow of the Phillips building.

"What do you want me to do about the fence?" Henley asked, pointing at the temporary barrier.

"What fence?" Kasey said, the corners of her mouth rising up into a grin.

"Roger that," Henley replied, dropping his foot down on the gas.

The armored carrier picked up speed, hurtling towards the aluminum barricade. Kasey had witnessed the Bearcat in action during the raid on the Marina. She knew the barrier didn't stand a chance.

The vehicle struck the barricade and obliterated it. The aluminum mesh exploded inward as the van burst through the cordon, dragging the fence along with it.

As they broke through, enormous hunks of welded steel rebar that had been connected like World War Two tank traps came into view. Several of them had been driven into the concrete. Others sat seemingly loose, scattered in front of the building. They were larger than Kasey had imagined and posed a more significant threat then the fence.

Henley swerved, pulling hard left on the wheel, narrowly avoiding the first of the tank traps. The hedge that had been planted to separate 432 Park Avenue from its neighbors fared poorly as Henley plowed a ten-foot-wide hole right through the middle of it. He stomped on the brakes as Kasey braced for impact. The Bearcat barely slowed as it approached a pair of roller doors on the adjoining building.

The steel roller doors fared little better than the hedge or the fence as the Bearcat punched straight through it, veered to the right, and into a BMW parked inside the private car park. The BMW crumpled like a sardine can as the Bearcat ground It into the wall. Kasey flew forward until her seat belt arrested her motion and she slammed back into the seat.

Shaking off the impact, she unclipped her belt and threw open the door. Henley grabbed a black tactical pack and clambered out of the cab, before looking at the crushed convertible.

"Someone's not going to be happy," Henley muttered.

Kasey looked around the private car park. There were more than a dozen luxury cars including a Bentley, a Ferrari, and a Lamborghini. "Oh, I dunno, Henley, in the scheme of things, you probably picked the cheapest of the lot. I'm sure West will be glad you missed the Bentley."

There was an almighty screech of twisted metal as the next armored carrier in the convoy struck the first of the tank traps. The steel, braced against the concrete, absorbed the brunt of the carrier's assault. Sparks leapt off the carrier as it ground to a halt. The next vehicle in the convoy veered right and slammed into the ground floor of the retail space on the right-hand side of 432 Park Avenue.

The fourth vehicle got caught in a tangled web of welded steel. With most of the sidewalk littered with stalled armored carriers, the convoy came to a halt and the rest of the strike force dismounted in the street itself.

Kasey followed Henley to the entrance of the parking garage.

A deafening rush filled the air. Looking up, she spotted the rocket's trail. Before it, a rocket-propelled grenade hurtled toward the convoy. The RPG struck the ground next to one of the Bearcats. The ballistic steel would take a fifty-caliber round but the high explosive ordnance lifted the vehicle, flipping it off its wheels and onto its side. Dust billowed out from the point of impact.

Gunfire erupted from above. Bullets slammed into the armored vehicles as the members of the strike force disembarked. Before her eyes, an ADI agent was dropped as fire from a high caliber rifle punched through him.

"It's an ambush," Kasey yelled. "They're above us. Get everyone into the target building!"

All about her, the strike force was in turmoil. Agents and NYPD officers huddled in the shadows of their armored vehicles. Akihiro's forces were everywhere, their elevated position giving them a deadly edge. If the strike force remained in the open, they would be slaughtered, and the attack would fail before it began.

Movement at the overturned transport caught her eye. As its rear doors opened, a sandy-haired figure stuck his head out.

Sanders.

Kasey glanced up. Opposite the Park Avenue superstructure was the modest Park Avenue Tower. Its lower terrace was providing Akihiro's disciples a lethal overwatch position.

With her hand raised to block the glare of the afternoon sun, Kasey searched for her quarry. She found him on the terrace among a handful of his companions. The disciple had an RPG tube standing before him that he was eagerly repacking.

"Up there." Kasey shouted pointing across the street. "We need to take him out before he reloads."

At her side, Morales raised his rifle and drew a bead on the position before opening fire.

Bullets stitched across the building's facade, but the elevated position made it difficult to hit their foe. The disciple simply dropped down and used the building itself as cover against the forces swarming beneath him.

Something moved on the roof top of the retail building. Lifting her gaze, Kasey realized a half a dozen of Akihiro's men were taking up positions. Gunfire split the air as the Shinigami's forces sprung their ambush. Glass rained down from above as more of his forces shattered windows of the surrounding buildings to allow themselves better vantage points.

We're surrounded. He knew we were coming. This isn't an ambush—it's a bloodbath.

Kasey watched as the first of Hades' dismounting Helldrakes was cut in half. The back door of the flipped troop carrier burst open and Sanders clambered out.

Kasey called into her transmitter. "Sanders, are you ok?"

"A bit shook up, but the carrier took the worst of it."

The strike force was pinned down and using the vehicles as cover, the strike force returned fire as best they could. Kasey cringed as she saw an officer of the Ninth Precinct fall, his Kevlar vest failing to save his life. A second later, the ADI agent at his side collapsed, blood pooling on the sidewalk beneath him.

"We need to get off the street. It's a killing ground," Kasey called into her earpiece.

"Easier said than done," Henley replied. "We may be concealed from the worst of it here. Only those across the street have any line of sight to us. We need to level the battlefield. If we can deal with that emplacement across the street, our forces will have some room to maneuver, but at the moment they are surrounded. It may only be thirty feet to the building, but it may as well be three hundred. If they break cover, they'll be cut down."

Kasey watched as two of the Shinigami disciples on the terrace stood and fired bursts into the strike force beneath. The dismounting agents took cover, but the disciple holding the RPG got to his feet.

He leveled the weapon at Sanders' already battered vehicle.

"Sanders, look out! RPG!" Kasey shouted, her voice shrill.

Sanders turned towards the RPG. With bullets dancing all around him, he raised his hands and chanted, *"Ahweorfan!"*

The rocket veered off course, as if it had a mind of its own. Instead of hurtling towards the Chancellor, it wheeled wildly to the right and slammed into the roof of the five-story retail building. The sniper's nest occupied by the Shinigami disciples was blown to smithereens.

With the right flank in shambles, the strike force had a little room to breathe.

"Dispatch. Where is our air support? We could really use it right about now," Kasey asked into her earpiece.

"Air support is inbound. Sixty seconds out," dispatch answered.

"I'm not sure we're going to make it that long. We need them now."

A spear of emerald energy hurtled down from above. An unfortunate Helldrake at Hades' flank was caught in the blast. The arcane energy stripped the flesh from his bones.

"There isn't enough cover," Sanders replied. "ADI, raise a shield."

The disembarking agents chanted as they wove their energy into a protective ward. The latticework of energy began to form above the armored carriers. As bullets struck the shield, bursts of light flickered across its surface. Under the safety of the protective shield, the strike force regathered. It wouldn't last long, though; the ward may have been robbing the bullets of their lethal kinetic energy, but each impact was draining energy from the wizards maintaining the shield. In time it would fail, leaving the strike force exposed once more.

In the shattered wreckage of the retail building's rooftop, there was movement. Several of the acolytes had survived the RPG and had resumed firing on the street below.

"Who was inside the transport that destroyed the store?" Kasey asked.

"That would be me," Bishop replied through the earpiece.

"I should have known," Kasey answered. "Couldn't resist a little window shopping, huh?"

"Would have been nice," Bishop replied, "but Thompkins managed to obliterate it, along with most of the first floor."

"A real shame, but there are still a few stragglers on the rooftop there that are making our life difficult. Think you could deal with them?"

"Already on our way," Bishop answered, panting. "Five floors of flaming stairs. Almost there, hang tight."

Before her eyes, an acolyte fell off the roof, plunging five floors to the street below. Moments later, Bishop and her team emerged and took up firing positions on top of the building.

The Shinigami acolytes opposite Park Avenue were emptying clip after clip into the strike force beneath. They weren't even trying to cover themselves now.

Kasey raised her hands and chanted, *"Egni Ysgarlad."*

A lance of scarlet energy, like a flaming sword, leapt from her palms. She guided it through their midst. The arcane energy sliced through them like they were paper, shearing their torsos from the rest of their bodies in one fell swoop.

The arcane energy swung toward the Shinigami that was reloading the RPG. It sliced straight through the weapon, detonating its payload. The resulting explosion silenced the Shinigami position for good.

Thumping rotor blades overhead signaled the arrival of precinct's air support. The aerial reinforcements bracketed the surrounding buildings with weapons fire.

"Let's move!" Kasey shouted.

With the officers overhead providing covering fire, Kasey, Henley, and the balance of the strike force ran for the protective shield the ADI had summoned. With dozens of wizards strengthening their shield, it held firm as the fire of the Shinigami forces slackened.

"Into the building!" Sanders called leading the charge into the building. "The sooner we're off the street, the better."

The strike force closed ranks and surged toward their objective; 432 Park Avenue was finally within reach. The covered windows may have concealed the buildings' interior from the outside world, but it still seemed more inviting than the bloodshed that had met them on the street.

"Dispatch, we're ready to breach," Kasey called. "Thanks for the aerial assist. If you could insert the tactical squads on the roof, we'll pincer them."

"Roger that," dispatch replied.

Both choppers began to climb, making their way to the towering rooftop of 432 Park Avenue.

"Dispatch, this is Aerial 2-4," a stern voice said through the earpiece. "We have someone on the roof."

"Take him out," Kasey bellowed.

"Kasey, this is Aerial 2-4. He's, uh, glowing."

Oh, no.

Kasey looked up to see a torrent of billowing emerald flames surge toward both helicopters. The first chopper veered violently to avoid the blaze but clipped its rotors on the Park Avenue skyscraper. The chopper crumpled as the arcane flames consumed the second helicopter, seizing its engines and likely immolating its crew.

Then, as swiftly as they had climbed, both helicopters began to fall.

CHAPTER 10

B oth helicopters fell from the sky, tumbling and turning through the air as they plunged twelve hundred feet to the ground.

"We've clipped the building. We're going down," one of the pilots shouted into his comms.

"Inside, now!" Kasey yelled, pushing those in front of her as they shoved their way through the narrow entrance into the building.

The first helicopter clipped the building once more, its rotors being annihilated by the building's unyielding facade. The second helicopter, which had been caught in the arcane conflagration, was silent as it dropped like a stone.

Kasey assessed her options. There was no saving the aerial borne tactical units. Those that survived the arcane assault would certainly perish in the crash. Kasey had to put her efforts into saving those on the ground around her. The debris from the falling helicopters posed a considerable threat to the strike force who were desperately fighting to get off the street.

As she reached the doorway, she turned and chanted *"Tarian!"*

A shimmering shield of sapphire energy rose from the sidewalk. Kasey raised her gaze and spotted the helicopters' sharp descent. Her heart pounded in her chest. It was a race, her rising shield against the falling aircraft, with her life hanging in the balance. She centered her mind and focused all of her will on the shield before her.

The first chopper veered wildly, as the pilot attempted to bring it down in the middle of the intersection of Madison and East 56th Street. His efforts were in vain as the helicopter nosedived at the last moment before slamming into the asphalt. The chopper crumpled in on itself. Sparks leapt as the tail rotors hit one of the intersection's many traffic lights, and a billowing fireball blossomed out from the shattered aircraft.

The other helicopter slammed into the roof of one of the convoy's parked Bearcat transports.

The falling chopper crushed the cab of the armored vehicle. Roaring fire played across its surface. The flickering orange flames battled with the emerald conflagration that had consumed the aircraft. A moment later, the helicopter and Bearcat exploded.

Kasey shielded her eyes as the detonation sent a shock wave rippling outward. Twisted metal ricocheted through the street, turning it into a death trap. The heat from the blast washed over her, buffeting against her shield. Fortunately, the arcane ward held firm against the shards of shrapnel that sliced into its shimmering surface. Were it not for the magical barrier, she would have been cut to shreds.

Opening her eyes, she examined the carnage around her.

Smoke rose from the ruined Bearcat, whilst the helicopter was scattered to the four corners of the street. The chopper's rear rotors had broken free, one of which had missed Kasey by mere feet. It sat buried in one of the ten-foot square windows that lined each of the faces of 432 Park Avenue. As Kasey looked closer, she could still see the emerald flames lapping along its surface. Whatever spell Akihiro had used on the aircraft, it was persistent and deadly. It appeared to have entirely consumed the crew before they even had a chance to scream.

Kasey's heart ached at the loss of life but there was nothing she could do for them now. Dropping her shield to preserve her strength, she turned and entered 432 Park Avenue to find the members of the strike force rallying.

Inside, Park Avenue was not what she'd expected. She had seen the towering residential complex in her visions numerous times in the last year. She had seen the attack on New York from every conceivable angle, but it still filled her with a surreal sensation to be here at its epicenter.

This is where it all begins. The one building that can withstand the devastation that Akihiro is about to unleash.

It was also perhaps the most dangerous place on earth. It was apparent that Akihiro was expecting them. They had charged head long into a war zone. The ambush on the street had already taken a toll on the strike force. They had lost almost a dozen people just to make it in the door. An unsettling lump in Kasey's throat told her that they would not be the last. Akihiro's acolytes had always proved themselves adept at selling their lives.

The first floor of the residential skyscraper was still unfinished. Pallets of tiles and steel piping cluttered the ground floor. A bank of elevators ran along one wall, while an emergency stairwell occupied the left corner of the room. The raised first floor ceilings were almost twenty feet off the ground, creating an illusion of spaciousness. While Park Avenue towered over the city, the skyscraper's footprint was surprisingly narrow.

"Spread out, secure the room. They well and truly know we are here now. We need to lock this building down," Sanders ordered.

"I will work with West to tighten the cordon," Bishop replied, via the comms. "This rooftop provides us with an excellent vantage point. No one will be able to slip in or out without us having a clean shot at them."

The other members of the strike force spread out to secure the first floor. Kasey studied the pallets of tiles. Rather than being stacked in a corner they ran in neat lines, forming a makeshift barrier. Odd, given that space was at a premium.

Oh, no.

The penny dropped as the Shinigami disciples rose up from behind the makeshift barrier and unleashed hell at point blank range.

"Down!" Kasey shouted, ducking behind a pillar.

The Shinigami opened fire and two police officers dropped immediately, followed by an ADI agent who was turning to face the new threat.

In the midst of the carnage, Hades didn't miss a step. He simply drew his pistols and went to work.

The Shinigami unleashed short bursts before ducking back behind the pallets to avoid the retaliatory fire from the strike force.

Hades wasn't having a bar of it; every time one of them raised their head to fire, Hades took it off. Both pistols blazed as Hades dropped four of the henchmen in quick succession. With each kill, the weight of fire from the right flank eased.

Their remaining comrades turned their weapons on Hades. He dove behind the pile of internal piping. The Shinigami poured round after round after Hades but to no avail. He pressed himself flat against the concrete floor as he reloaded his pistols. Bullets ricocheted off the steel piping, but Hades appeared to have a sixth sense for when to keep his head down. Unfortunately, he was trapped, pinned down by the remaining acolytes.

Zryx held up her fist, signaling the Helldrakes to assault the Shinigami position. Breaking cover the Helldrakes' coordinated fire drove the Shinigami into cover. She leapt deftly onto the pallet of tiles and raised her submachine gun before proceeding to cut down the remaining ambushers in a withering hail of automatic weapons fire. Hades' pet may have been psychotic, but she was also fearless. Even when facing a storm of firepower, she cut down the Shinigami acolytes with ruthless and clinical efficiency.

As the gunfire eased, there was the dull scrape of steel on steel. Kasey turned to one of the elevators beside the Helldrakes.

As the doors parted, they revealed a weapons crew manning a .50 Caliber heavy machine gun. Akihiro had turned the elevator into a weapons emplacement. Fortified and dug in like a makeshift bunker, the weapons team had a perfect arc of fire.

Zryx dove off the pallet as the heavy weapons team pulled the trigger. The machine gun roared to life. At point blank range, the Helldrakes had nowhere to go. The machine gun cut through five of them before they could process its existence. As the remaining Helldrakes scattered, the weapons team turned the machine gun on the remainder of the strike force.

The strike force unloaded their weapons at the heavy machine gun team. Unfortunately, the steel plates that had been welded together as a makeshift barrier were proving highly effective at keeping the weapons team alive. Every second they survived, more of the strike force fell.

An ADI agent at Kasey's right hurled a sphere of fire at the elevator. The blaze struck the wall, super heating the steel. It glowed an angry shade of scarlet but still the weapon blazed away.

As the weapons team brought the heavy machine-gun to bear on the ADI contingent, Sanders emerged from behind the next pillar, raised both hands and chanted, *"Drifan!"*

The incantation leapt from his outstretched hands. It closed the short distance between him and the elevator swifter than the eye could track it. The spell hit the Shinigami position with unyielding force. The improvised fortification was cleft in twain, the blast carving a hole through the heavy machine-gun, the weapons crew, and the elevator itself. When the dust cleared, sunlight was streaming in through the gaping rend in the elevator shaft's external wall.

The last of the ambushing acolytes were dispatched by the strike force's relentless advance, and the lobby fell silent.

Kasey surveyed the damage. The Helldrakes were tending to their wounded. At least four of them were dead, and another was critically injured. The heavy machine gun had reaped a fearsome toll. Among the fallen was a sandy-haired police officer from the Ninth Precinct and an ADI agent that Kasey didn't recognize. There were at least four other wounded members of the strike force being attended to by their comrades.

"See to our wounded," Kasey directed as she bent down to examine a wounded police officer. "Get them to the safety of the cordon and lock this place down. Check the other elevator shafts, ensure there aren't any other surprises waiting for us in there."

Sanders and the other agents moved through the ground floor, sweeping for any remaining acolytes. The strike force had not held back; the acolytes had been exterminated with extreme prejudice. Hades and the Helldrakes prized open the remaining elevator shafts, one at a time. They were empty except for a singular shaft that held a functioning elevator.

"Kasey, this one isn't empty," Hades called out. "There's a working elevator here, and we all know that Akihiro is up there. That was him that took down the choppers. So let's take a ride. We can end this right now."

Kasey shook her head. "That's not a ride, it's a death sentence. If we step into that coffin, there isn't a chance in hell we make it safely to the top."

"Hell's my domain, Chase. You'll be surprised what I can make happen with a chance," Hades countered.

"Not now, Hades. When we do go after him, we'll be taking the stairs. You saw what happened to the choppers. Unless you want to join them in the next life, you'll need to keep your feet on solid ground. Besides, we deal with the weapon first, then we clear the building, floor by floor and cut him out like the cancer that he is. Understood?"

"Kasey is right," Sanders replied as he checked behind the pallets for anyone else who might be lying in wait. "As much as

I can't believe I'm saying this, Akihiro is the lesser evil here. That weapon is going to wipe out everyone in the city. Nothing else matters until we disable it."

"Exactly, that's why we need you to hold down the fort here, Hades." Kasey said, rising to her feet. "Sanders and I are taking our units and going after the weapon. When Akihiro realizes what we are doing, him and whatever forces he has with him are likely to try and stop us. We need you to prevent any reinforcements from reaching us. Can you stick to the plan?"

Hades holstered the pistol in his right hand. "Fine. We'll hold down the fort, but if Akihiro shows his face, I'm not making any promises. We'll start the party with or without you."

"Fair enough," Kasey said, scratching at the nape of her neck. "As long as he doesn't make it out of the building, I don't care who gets to kill him."

"Very well then. We have an understanding," Hades said. "We'll hold down the fort here while you deal with the weapon. Don't drag your feet."

"Agreed. It's time to move out. Sanders, Morales, Henley, let's move," Kasey answered.

"Ready when you are, Chase," Morales replied, striding over from the bank of elevators. "Where do we start?"

Henley fell in behind them, still wearing the black tactical pack he'd dragged out of the crashed bearcat.

"The stairs," Kasey replied. "The weapon is somewhere beneath us, in the foundations, so down we go."

As the strike force fell into step behind her, Kasey led the charge for the stairs. Reaching the landing, she let out a sigh.

More stairs. Gee, I hate the stairs.

It had been a hell of a day, from waking up in the Administorum, to the Night Crew assault on the precinct, and now taking on Akihiro. She could feel the fatigue building in her limbs but forced herself to ignore it. She plunged down the stairs, taking them two at a time as she focused her mind on the task at hand. Somewhere beneath her was a weapon that could level the city but knowing that it existed and knowing how to find it were two wildly different matters.

According to Vida's estimation, the foundations themselves, while deep, would not be nearly enough to detonate the weapon and trigger the seismic activity Kasey had witnessed in her visions. A single blast wouldn't be enough to wipe out the city. Not unless that singular blast was targeted with pinpoint precision.

Vida had used the city's geological records to identify the most likely target of opportunity for the weapon. The bedrock beneath New York City was made up of a wide array of rock formations, among them serpentinite. Large deposits of the green-tinged stone were found all throughout the ground beneath the city. The stone itself was less dense than granite and, according to Vida, a large deposit of serpentinite rested against Manhattan's own fault line. Vida surmised that it was the position of the serpentinite deposit on the fault line that made it the most likely target for the Shinigami weapon. Upon detonation, the weapon would vaporize the serpentinite deposit, agitate the fault line, and set off a chain reaction of seismic destruction that would destroy the city.

The fault line ran through Manhattan and the deposit in question was almost a mile from Park Avenue, meaning that the Shinigami would have needed to begin boring a tunnel months ago. If the weapon was to be detonated today, most of the tunnel had already been dug. The thought of needing to run a literal mile in her current state was a less than appealing prospect. Right now, more than anything else, she needed to find the entrance to that tunnel, or everything she had done, every struggle she'd endured, would be in vain.

Down and down the stairs wound, as they plunged deeper and deeper into the earth. The air seemed to grow thicker and thicker as they descended beneath the earth. Kasey swallowed in an attempt to ease the pressure on her ear drums. She lost count of just how many flights of stairs she had descended when abruptly they came to an end, opening onto a landing that led into a vast chamber. Enormous pillars ran from floor to ceiling, each of them as wide as Kasey was tall. The ceiling was almost twenty feet above their head with rows of LEDs illuminating the hall. On closer inspection, Kasey realized the pillars actually ran through the ceiling.

They're the building's foundations.

Sanders caught up with her. "Careful, Kasey, it could be another trap."

Kasey nodded but proceeded into the chamber anyway. Raising her hands, she summoned her power, ready to unleash it on a moment's notice.

She searched the chamber as she made her way down the vast aisle that ran between the pillars. Scrap materials and discarded tools littered the floor. The room was quiet, but for the strike force behind her. She could hear Sanders and the agents fanning out to search the cavernous room.

She walked the length of the chamber, but when she reached the other end, she'd found nothing of note. There wasn't a single Shinigami acolyte to be seen anywhere. Moreover, there wasn't a door, access ladder, or passageway. The entire subbasement of Park Avenue appeared to have been sealed tight.

"Sanders, have you found anything?" Kasey called out.

"Nothing yet. I don't know what I was expecting," Sanders replied, "but I was certainly expecting something."

"Me too," Kasey said, doubling back. "You think it's possible that perhaps it was once open, but now that it has served its purpose, they have gone ahead and sealed whatever passage they used to keep the device concealed?"

Sanders shook his head, "The tunneling is a slow process. They would have been at it for months now. If they had tried to do it too quickly, the city would have detected the seismic disturbance. No, there is far too great a margin for error. Drills burn out, machines need maintenance. There is no way that Akihiro would have sealed the tunnel until he was certain that the device would function as intended. There has to be some way to reach it, just in case. There must be something we are missing."

Kasey studied the walls. They were made of double-stacked bricks from floor to ceiling. They had not been painted over or sealed. She examined the grout between the rows of bricks, but the patterns seemed to be in order. No obvious gateway or passage that she could see.

Searching the entire chamber, brick by brick, for a hidden passage or trapdoor could take hours. Time she didn't have.

"Kasey. What do you think the chances are that there is an access way inside one of these pillars?" Sanders asked. "Originally, I figured that they were all support pillars, the foundations for the building above us. But there is always a chance that one of them hides a ladder or something that will take us farther beneath the surface."

"Well, I have nothing, so let's get looking," Kasey replied. "There are dozens of them, so we'll need to fan out and check."

Kasey and the agents spread out, forming a line across the subbasement.

Kasey approached the first pillar. It was an immense cylindrical steel framework into which concrete had been poured during the construction. Kasey felt her way around the edges of the support, looking for any sign that might indicate a trapdoor or passageway.

Sanders was right: it would be simple to hide a ladder inside one of them. If the shafts and supports ran vertically through the floor, who would suspect that one of them was empty? Kasey made her way around the column.

Nothing.

She pounded on the steel, just in case. It was solid.

"What are you doing?" Henley called.

"If there is a ladder inside, it would have to be hollow. Just testing to be sure," she said.

Not to be discouraged, she hurried to the next and repeated her examination. Feeling around the structural support, she searched for a seam or hinge, anything that might reveal a hidden door.

Again, nothing.

She gave an exasperated sigh and moved on to the next pillar. As she made her way through the chamber, she found nothing out of the ordinary. Each pillar was just like the last, nothing more or less than the foundations to the building itself.

"Find anything, Sanders?" Kasey asked. "Coming up empty here."

"Me too," Sanders replied. "Nothing at all."

Kasey approached the last support. It was right beside the stairs that led back up to the ground floor. Its exterior matched the others but as Kasey made her way around the column, she spotted a second seam in the steel. It was faint, and it ran parallel to the first. As Kasey followed the line, she realized that above her head, a third line joined the two seems together. Together, they could form a doorway.

She struck the steel. The noise reverberated through the column.

It's hollow.

"Sanders, get over here," she yelled, pushing at the door. "I think I found something."

The strike force raced over to the pillar, Sanders at their head.

He stepped up beside her. "What have you got?"

She pointed at the pillar. "These seams. The other pillars only have a single seam. So, I thought it might be a hidden door. I just can't seem to shift it though."

Sanders tried to use his hands to prize open the door, but it wouldn't budge.

Kasey turned and roamed through the room, searching the scraps littering the floor. Finding a piece of broken steel, she snatched it up and then ran back to the pillar. She stuck the end of the steel into the seam and attempted to use it as a crowbar to open the column, but she couldn't budge it.

"Maybe it's an arcane passage," Sanders suggested. "Perhaps we need to use magic to open it."

Kasey paused, steel beam in hand. "That makes sense. Akihiro wouldn't want anyone finding it by accident. An arcane enchantment would certainly keep it safe from unwanted visitors."

Sanders raised his hands and chanted, *"Feldlaes."*

Nothing happened.

"I've had about enough of this," Sanders said with a scowl.

They were nearly out of time. Kasey resisted checking the clock on her phone. She didn't want to know how closely they were cutting it.

"Maybe it's nothing," she replied, dropping the steel. "I felt certain it was something. But maybe I was just wrong."

"There is only one way to find out," Sanders said. He closed his eyes and chanted, *"Windgerest."*

He clenched his fists as if he were trying to squish something.

There was a howling shriek as the steel buckled. The edges of the panel started to twist and contort.

"Sanders, it's working. Keep it up," she shouted, slapping him on the back.

A bead of sweat ran down Sanders' brow as he continued to channel his energy into the panel. Kasey could feel the arcane exertion as Sanders bent the elements to his will.

The panel buckled. The sheet steel gave off a tortured shriek as it rolled back like a can being opened. As the panel contorted, it revealed an enormous cavity in the pillar.

Inside, instead of a ladder, was a stack of C4 explosives.

"Stop!" Kasey shouted.

Sanders released his incantation as the steel panel broke free and dropped to the floor, a twisted wreck.

He turned to Kasey. "What?"

"Look!" Kasey replied, pointing at the cavern inside the support column.

The C4 was stacked from the floor to Kasey's eye level, their priming caps wired together and linked to a central control panel. A flashing red light was all the warning Kasey needed to know that was active.

"That's what I was worried about," Kasey replied. "If you set that off, we're all dead."

Sanders shook his head as he studied the mountain of explosives. "Why are they in here, though? I thought you said the explosion had to be much deeper beneath the surface. Surely triggering this device would only serve to destroy this building."

Kasey bit her lip. "Yeah, you're right. This would bring down Park Avenue, maybe a few of the surrounding buildings, but it won't level the city. I don't think this is the weapon that Akihiro is trying to guard.

"Perhaps he plans to use this to demolish the building after the attack on the city. Detonating that much explosive here in its foundations would sever its supports and surely bring it down. Perhaps it's a ploy to cover his tracks. Whatever his intentions are, we can't leave it here. If he sets that off, it'll kill all of us."

Together, Kasey and Sanders stood shoulder to shoulder, silently staring at the flashing mountain of explosives before them.

As Kasey pondered her next move, she ground her teeth together. All her visions of the attack had led them here. Vida's research had brought them to this chamber. Everything they knew about the attack had brought them here to this place now.

They had only found a pile of explosives that would level one building, though.

Is it possible we are in the wrong place?

Kasey shook off the thought. The attack on the helicopters proved that Akihiro was inside Park Avenue. If he was here, the weapon would be too. Akihiro would want to be at the epicenter of the chaos to harness the life force of the city's inhabitants as they expired.

It can't be a coincidence. It must be here somewhere. Somewhere beneath this building, there has to be a tunnel.

"Is it possible that the access point is underneath the explosives and Akihiro is simply trying to make it difficult for us to follow?" Sanders asked.

Kasey nodded. "It's definitely possible. There could be some kind of access way beneath this device."

Motioning to the Ninth Precinct bomb squad technicians, Kasey pointed at the device. "Can you defuse that?"

The technician approached the pillar and studied the cavity and its contents.

"I should be able to. If we remove the detonators, the explosives themselves are harmless enough. I don't think he ever meant for this device to be found. There are no tamper switches or safeguards in place. Give me a few minutes, and I can render the device safe."

"Okay. Get to work. I don't want to put too fine a point on this, but we are running out of time," Kasey replied.

The technician looked Kasey in the eyes. "With the greatest respect, Chase, one mistake here and we'll all be out of time. The biggest worry is what happens if he decides to trigger it before we can defuse the device. One radio signal and we're all toast."

"I wouldn't worry about that," Henley said from behind them. "That's why West had me bring this."

Kasey turned as he patted the tactical pack he'd been carrying since the strike force set out.

"It's a frequency jammer," he said. "It should stop any signal that might detonate the device. The Chief thought it might come in handy."

"Should?" Kasey asked as her heart began beating a little quicker.

Henley nodded, but Kasey took little comfort from the response.

Turning to the technician, she continued, "If you could disarm the device before we have to test that theory, it would be marvelous."

Stepping away from the pillar, she tried to get her emotions under control.

The technician crouched down and began to examine the space more closely. He traced his fingers along the wires as he tracked the labyrinthine connections between them. Identifying all of the blasting caps, he traced them back to a central receiver. Then he pulled out a pair of wire cutters from his belt and, with a deep breath, cut the wire.

The building heaved so violently that Kasey was thrown into Sanders. They tumbled to the floor as the building shook in protest. All around her, the strike force was falling over themselves as a deafening rumble rolled through the chamber. With each shake, the building's structural supports heaved and groaned.

Oh, no. This is it. Kasey struggled to her knees. *We were too late. It has already begun.*

CHAPTER 11

The earth shook beneath them, and then as suddenly as it had begun, the tremors ceased.

The chamber grew still and Kasey struggled to her feet.

"What was that? What's going on down there?" Bishop's voice crackled through the earpiece.

"We're okay," Kasey replied, staring down the chamber. "I thought the weapon had detonated, but it seems I was mistaken."

"Whatever that earthquake was, it shook the whole block," Bishop said.

Kasey exhaled as she tried to calm her racing heart. "That's exactly what it was, Bishop. An earthquake. They're drilling toward the fault line. They must have triggered some tremors."

"You sound relieved," Sanders interjected.

"Well, first off, it wasn't the weapon, so it means we still have time. Second, did you hear that racket? It rolled through the basement like thunder, but it didn't come from beneath us, it came from over there." Kasey pointed through the cavernous chamber. "Don't you think it's odd that the building's foundations pass through this room, and yet there is this large aisle running between the pillars? It leads directly to that wall. Why leave a space that large unless it was needed for something? I think they built the machine right here. This is where the tunnel started."

Sanders nodded as he studied the space. "If that's the case, where is the tunnel now?"

Kasey pointed at the wall. "It's right there, hiding in plain sight. Just like Akihiro was." She raised her hand in front of her and chanted, "*Pêl Tân.*"

A wisp of flames flickered into being above her outstretched hand. With practiced art, she poured energy into the enchantment. The wisp grew, and soon a broiling ball of flames hovered in the air before her. Channeling her will, she hurled the ball of fire at the far wall. The flames hurtled through the room before striking the brick wall.

When they hit it, the spell's structure collapsed, and the flames washed over the exterior of the brick. As the spell licked at the surface, the wall shimmered and went translucent. The fire played across the clear facing, illuminating the chamber that lay beyond. The flames flickered and died, leaving the shimmering barrier intact. As the last vestiges of Kasey's spell faded, the wall flickered and the brick pattern emerged once more, leaving the illusion of a wall where the barrier divided the subbasement from the tunnel beyond.

Kasey stared at the brick wall. The scale of Akihiro's illusory barrier was staggering. The entire wall of the chamber itself was actually some kind of enchantment.

"Morales, you keep a lookout while the technician dismantles that C4. The rest of you, let's go." Kasey led the strike force back through the immense subbasement.

Reaching the illusion, she weighed her options. At a glance, she wasn't sure what type of ward Akihiro had conjured. Was it simply an optical illusion? Or was it actually a barrier that would prevent them from gaining entrance to the tunnel beyond?

Not willing to leave anything to chance, Kasey picked up a loose brick and hurled it at the wall. When the brick struck the wall, the surface shimmered, a series of ripples radiating out from the point of impact. For a passing moment, the place where the brick had impacted the wall became translucent, revealing the enormous tunnel leading away from the chamber.

Then, as quickly as they had appeared, the ripples ceased, and the wall appeared as it had before: a normal unassuming brick wall.

The brick Kasey had thrown landed back at her feet. The fact the brick had bounced back meant that the conjuration wasn't simply an illusion—it was a barrier. There was no way of telling exactly what might happen if she touched it and yet if they wanted to reach the tunnel, they were going have to pass through it.

"It's an enchantment," Sanders said from nearby. "Just like any other, it can only take so much punishment. We need to destroy it."

"What are you suggesting?" Kasey asked as she turned to face him.

"Direct assault," Sanders answered. "There is no way that barrier can stand up to a sustained attack from all of us. If we bring enough firepower to bear on it, we will drain its power source and it will collapse on itself." He glanced at his team. "Ready yourselves, agents. On my mark."

The ADI agents drew deep, summoning their power. Kasey could feel it immediately, the steady thrum of arcane energy building in the chamber. It was as if the area itself was electrified. The combined might of so many magical beings was intense.

" *Bael!*" Sanders chanted.

Torrents of fire leapt from his outstretched hands. The firestorm bathed the wall in an instant inferno. The barrier flickered as the fire played across its surface, but nonetheless it held firm against the assault.

Lightning arced at the barrier as another agent joined Sanders. The lightning raced across the barrier before earthing itself in the dirt. Next, dozens of lances of arcane energy of every hue and color struck the barrier, carving into it like a barrage of arcane lasers. The barrier glowed as its enchantment bowed under the arcane assault.

The illusion flickered. The bricks disappeared completely from sight as the enchanted wall faltered and then collapsed in on itself in a blinding flash of energy.

Kasey shielded her eyes. When she looked again, the tunnel stood before her, more than twenty feet in diameter. It ran away from the subbasement.

A narrow strip of lighting hung from the roof, casting a dim glow along the subterranean accessway.

Sanders raised his hand and the ADI ceased their assault.

Kasey approached the tunnel. She stepped forward onto the dirt and then crouched down to examine it. Two deep rows of tread marks ran into the tunnel, almost twelve feet apart.

"Sanders, check this out," she said without looking up. "These have to have come from the machine doing the boring for them. You can see the trail its left right here."

Sanders ducked down beside her. "Yup, Akihiro is definitely a clever cookie. He must've known that he couldn't use magic to carve the tunnel. It would have been too much energy to escape the Arcane Council's notice. Particularly this deep beneath the earth, we would have been immediately suspicious of it. Using a machine allowed him to escape detection. At any given time, there is boring going on beneath the city. It would be easy to camouflage his intentions here. Look, you can see where they have braced the tunnel as they have gone."

He pointed at the steel framework that braced the walls and roof of the tunnel to ensure it didn't collapse.

"Well, we have what we were looking for," Kasey said, standing. "These tracks will lead us straight to wherever the machine is. I'll bet that tremor was Akihiro accelerating his plan. He knows we have breached the building. We need to stop that machine before he can detonate its payload."

"You're going to go down there?" Henley asked.

Kasey shot him a sideways look. "Don't tell me you're afraid of the dark there, big guy."

He fidgeted as he shook his head. "Don't be silly, it's not the dark—it's the confined spaces that do it for me. I've never been a fan. The thought of that much ground on top of me, it's difficult to breathe." He sucked in a deep breath. "One thing goes wrong, and we could all be buried alive."

Kasey nodded. "I guess we better tread carefully then. Come on, let's go. The sooner we stop it, the sooner we can get the hell out of here."

Henley exhaled loudly as he followed her into the tunnel.

In her heart, she didn't blame them. They were hundreds of feet beneath the ground, in a makeshift tunnel dug by a lunatic who had every intention of blowing it up and bringing the city crashing down on top of it. If they were too late, they would all be dead.

She took a deep breath of her own to calm her racing heart, but it was in vain.

She was too close to calm down. The adrenaline pumped through her veins as she lengthened her pace, plunging deeper into the tunnel.

The underground passageway thrust downward. The angle of the descent was almost thirty degrees. Over the mile of its length, the downward descent would give it the extra depth Akihiro needed to reach the serpentinite deposit.

Vida's guess had been spot on. He was uncannily intuitive. No doubt if they lived through the ordeal, Kasey would never hear the end of his gloating.

As they descended deeper into the tunnel beneath New York City, a steady thrum filled the air. It seemed to grow in volume with every step forward.

"That'll be the machine," Sanders said. "We must be getting close."

The entire tunnel seemed to vibrate. The machine was definitely hard at work, moving inexorably toward its destination.

"We have to pick up the pace," Kasey replied. "Any moment now, they could detonate the weapon. Even if we were to stop it short of its destination, who knows how much damage it would still do."

She picked up her pace until she was almost running. Unlike the subbasement, the floor of the tunnel remained unfinished. It was largely gravel, rocks, and dirt that had been compacted as the bulky machine had passed over it. One misstep would see her on her ass, and a twisted ankle was a fate she just could not afford.

Even as the thought passed through her mind, she slipped on a loose rock. The rock shot down the tunnel and her legs went out from under her. She slammed onto her butt and slid down the incline. Her arms flailed outward, trying to slow her descent. Gravel dug at her skin.

Finally, she ground to a halt.

When she opened her eyes, she found Sanders standing over her with his hand outstretched.

"Are you okay?" he asked, peering down at her.

"Yeah, I'm fine. It's mostly my ego that's bruised."

She grabbed Sanders' hand, and he pulled her to her feet. She took a step but her tailbone groaned its protest.

"On second thought, I'm still a little bit tender," she replied.

"Need a hand?" Henley asked, appearing beside Sanders.

Kasey shook her head. "It's all good. It's going to take more than a few bruises and a hurt ego to stop me now."

Resuming a more measured pace, the strike force continued down the tunnel.

The tunneling sound ahead grew louder and louder. Kasey knew they must be nearing their mark, but it was difficult to measure distance in the semi-darkness.

She was so focused on her target, the tunnel boring machine, that she missed the black-clad assassins that emerged from the shadows.

The Shinigami acolytes materialized like wraiths. It was only the light reflecting off a raised blade that caught Kasey's eye.

Kasey whirled as the wickedly curved blade closed at her throat.

"Kasey, look out!" Henley called.

Time slowed as the blade arced toward her exposed throat.

The assassin was close, too close to duck; she would end up taking the blade in her face. Instead, she threw her arms up, a last-ditch attempt to save her exposed neck from the blade. A sharp sting shot through her as the blade bit into her forearm.

Then, out of nowhere, a shadow shot past Kasey.

Like a rampaging bull, it crashed into the assassin, wrenching the blade away before it could cut too deeply.

The assassin hit the ground hard with Henley on top of him. The assassin raised the blade as Henley drew back his fist. Henley's jab thundered into the assailant's face. The knife dropped from his hand as he collapsed unconscious.

Other Shinigami acolytes materialized from the darkness. They launched themselves at the strike force without a word. With the sound of the machine drowning out the melee in the tunnel, the assailants drew knives and pistols as the tunnel brawl devolved into close quarters fighting.

Kasey ducked an assassin that was swinging wildly in an attempt to take off her head. Grabbing the assassin's shoulders, she drove her knee straight into his crotch. As the man buckled over, Kasey wrenched the knife from his hand and threw it at another acolyte that was charging toward her. The blade turned as it sliced through the air before coming to a halt, blade first as it lodged in the man's chest. The Shinigami dropped to his knees gasping for air, likely the result of a punctured lung.

Kasey changed her grip on the Shinigami in her hands and broke his neck as a beam of arcane energy sliced past her. The spell bore straight through a Shinigami acolyte before tracing a blazing trail along the tunnel wall. It sheared clean through a support beam. A three-foot section of the beam broke free and fell to the ground with a thud. Dirt and dust rained down from the ceiling as the tunnel threatened to collapse.

"No magic!" Kasey shouted at the agent who had cast the spell. "You'll bring the whole tunnel down on top of us. That's why they're only using their knives. They don't want to risk bringing down the tunnel."

The ADI agent nodded and drew his pistol.

Kasey turned back to the task at hand. The Shinigami flooded toward them in a mass of bodies and blades. As she readied herself, the lead Shinigami raised a pistol. The steel barrel was leveled directly at her. At this distance, he wouldn't miss.

She stared down the jet-black barrel and began to chant. She prayed the defensive ward would form in time but before she could finish the words, the Shinigami's head exploded. Kasey glanced back to see Sanders with this service weapon raised. Thin wisps of smoke rose from its barrel.

Kasey nodded her appreciation before throwing herself back into the fray. It was close quarters tunnel fighting at its deadliest. Pistols barked as they fired, the gunshots puncturing through the incessant whirring of the tunnel boring machine.

In the swirling melee, it was difficult to distinguish friend from foe.

The next Shinigami she came face to face with, she grabbed his wrist and drove it into her knee. He dropped his knife but reached for a holster at the small of his back. As he drew his pistol, Kasey grabbed his wrist and twisted it. She wrenched the weapon from his grasp, then pistol whipped him with bone-shattering force. His head snapped around like a rag doll before he dropped to the floor unconscious. Changing her grip, Kasey emptied the pistol into the charging Shinigami, bringing down three more of them. As the weapon clicked empty, she hurled it straight at the head of the fourth Shinigami who was struggling over the bodies of his fallen comrades.

Kasey ducked under the man's right jab, but he reached out and grabbed her with his left hand. As Kasey struggled to break his grip he doubled down, grabbing Kasey in a complete bear hug. Kasey stomped on his foot in an effort to loosen his grasp, but the hulking bear of a man simply squeezed her tighter. With a grunt, he lifted her clear off the ground.

Kasey squirmed and struggled to be free of him, but the thug hurled her at the ground. She shielded her head to cushion her fall. If she struck a rock, she could easily be knocked unconscious, and in the murderous confines of the tunnel that would mean certain death at the hands of the Shinigami acolytes.

She hit the ground hard, gasping as the air was driven from her lungs. She fought for her breath as the Shinigami loomed over her. His brown eyes stared into hers with utter contempt. When Kasey tried to rise, he drove a punishing boot into her kidneys. Kasey rolled with the blow but still it hurt like hell. She groaned in pain as the Shinigami drew back to sink his boot in once more. She couldn't take another blow. She lunged out with her right leg, putting everything she had into the kick. Her boot connected with the side of the Shinigami's knee.

Her mouth turned up in satisfaction as she heard the joint shatter with a sickening crunch the Shinigami collapsed to the ground. Kasey rolled on top of him and punched him in the face. The Shinigami was dazed but still managed to wrap his big meaty hands around her windpipe and squeeze.

Kasey searched about desperately with her hands. Feeling something hard, she closed her fingers around the rock. She lifted it and slammed it into his face. The Shinigami's arms went slack as he lost consciousness. From the blood streaming down his face, Kasey suspected he was about to lose his life.

There was no time for pity though. Kasey shoved the bleeding body aside and struggled to her feet. She surveyed the swirling melee.

All about her, the ADI were locked in a struggle against the Shinigami. It was difficult to discern just how many Shinigami were in the tunnel, but when Kasey considered those that they had dispatched upstairs, and on the street outside, she knew that they had woefully miscalculated the amount of support Akihiro had at his disposal. Kasey could feel her hope hanging by a thread. They were so close to the machine, and yet for everything she had been through, for every agonizing inch of ground that they had gained, it felt like it would never be enough.

You can't think like that. Your entire life, you have been seeing this damn attack. The visions, being hunted by the Shinigami, it had all led you here. Millions of lives hang in the balance and they're all counting on you. So, stop feeling so damn sorry for yourself, and kick their asses.

Kasey threw herself back into the fray with renewed vigor. The first Shinigami to come within her reach took a throat punch for his efforts. While the acolyte struggled for breath, Kasey grabbed his hand, twisted his wrist, and fired the pistol straight through his chest. As he dropped, Kasey wrenched the pistol from his grasp.

The next Shinigami took a double tap to the chest and collapsed, gurgling as he went down. Reaching down, Kasey relieved him of his weapon also.

Armed with a pistol in each hand, she worked her way through the melee. Henley struggled with two Shinigami pinning him down. One of them raised his blade and drove it into Henley's chest. As the blade struck the Kevlar, it snapped at the hilt. The Shinigami recoiled, still brandishing the broken blade, and lunged for Henley's face.

Kasey's pistol was faster, dropping the murderous Shinigami with a single shot to the head. A moment later, the second Shinigami joined his friend in the realm of the departed.

Kasey moved through the battle, emptying the magazine into the Shinigami at point-blank range. When the pistols ran dry, she grabbed the next Shinigami to come within range and hurled him into the wall. He slammed into the steel support and as he bounced off, Kasey coat-hangered him to the ground. Following him down, she wrapped herself around him in a sleeper grip, slowly and purposefully tightening her grasp. He fought against her grasp, but as the seconds crawled by, Kasey felt him go limp in her arms.

She hunted for her next victim, but there was none.

As suddenly as it had begun, the fight was over. Kasey hurled the unconscious Shinigami out of her path and got to her feet.

Sanders strode over to her. His eyes were wide, and his brow was deeply furrowed.

Kasey knew that look; he was worried.

He stopped in front of her. "Kasey, are you okay? You're covered in blood."

She looked down and realized it was true. Lancets of her own blood ran down her arms, the results of the first assailant's knife. Her clothes were covered in dust and blood from the Shinigami ambush. She wiped her brow and her hand came away red. Feeling at her head, she searched for the wound but found none.

Relieved, she replied, "Don't worry, Sanders, it's not mine. At least not for the most part. We need to keep moving though. We're almost out of time."

As if in agreement, the tunnel shuddered as another tremor ran through it.

"Alright," Sanders replied, gesturing toward her. "Lead the way."

CHAPTER 12

Kasey charged down the tunnel. The vibrations continued to intensify as she descended, the strike force right behind her. With the Shinigami ambush dispatched, they made swift progress on their descent.

The grinding noise from the tunnel boring machine grew until they were able to hear nothing else.

Sweat ran down her brow, not only from her exertion but from the temperature in the tunnel. It seemed to rise the farther they went. The beads of sweat ran down her face and off her cheek, before landing on her bullet-proof vest. She strove to pace herself and control her breathing. She'd spent enough time running to know that the more oxygen she was able to pump to her exhausted extremities, the better her limbs would respond to combat the buildup of lactic acid.

Up ahead, a glimmer of silver caught her eye.

It's the machine.

She glanced back over her shoulder. Sanders was right behind her as were the other agents. Henley loped along behind them, bringing up the rear. The enormous backpack he carried with him brought Kasey comfort. The signal jammer would hopefully prevent Akihiro from detonating the device entirely. For a moment, Kasey imagined the look on his face as he pressed the button to activate the device but nothing happened. Years of his life had been poured into bringing this plan to fruition. He'd spent years gambling that he would be able to stay the hand of death indefinitely. His agitation would be extreme, and his response would be deadly. He couldn't make it out of the building alive.

As she drew nearer to the machine, the size of it boggled her mind. The monstrosity filled the entire tunnel. It was almost twenty feet wide, and almost as tall. It rumbled forward on two sets of rotating tracks. Dirt and stone from the bore were being funneled to the sides before being ejected behind the machine.

Seeing her target within reach, she picked up her pace, anxious to catch the vehicle as it continued to roll forward. Slowly but surely, it ground away at the tunnel ahead. The noise was deafening, and not for the first time, Kasey wished she had earplugs to dampen the noise. Their plan had been focused on finding the device, not their personal comfort while doing so.

A set of steel rungs ran up the back of the machine. Kasey reached for them. She halted as a Shinigami stood up on top of the machine. From his perch above the steel monstrosity, he raised his assault rifle and took aim at Kasey.

Kasey dove forward, aiming to shield herself with the body of the machine. As she dove, she tucked and rolled to protect her head from the worst of the fall.

The gunshots punctured through the incessant grinding of the bore, but the first bullet passed inches from her leg as she slid beneath the bulk of the machine.

From her place in the crawlspace beneath the tunnel borer, she could make out the ADI's response. Sanders and the agents behind him raised their weapons. They blasted away at the Shinigami in a deadly rain of fire. A second later, the black-clad body slammed into the tunnel floor behind the machine.

Another one bites the dust.

Kasey considered emerging from her hidey hole, but in the event that the Shinigami had any other companions waiting, she preferred to take a less expected route. Shielded from prying eyes by the bulk of the machine, she crawled forward, searching the underside of the boring machine for any form of access hatch, or entrance that might lead into the machine. She scrambled forward on her hands and knees, racing against the machine's slow but unyielding progress.

Reaching the front of the machine, she saw the bore for the first time.

The immense rotating tunnel bore was carving through the stone, breaking it up and grinding it to dust before funneling it behind the machine. The bore filled the entire circumference of the tunnel; there was no going around it. If Kasey wanted to get inside the machine, she would have to crawl through the narrow space between the front of the tracks and the start of the bore.

She turned around and scanned the bottom of the machine again until she was satisfied there was no other choice. There wasn't a hatch or access point to be found anywhere.

With her options limited, she edged forward, finding a space between the rotating tread of the machine and the tunnel bore that was drilling away. There were only a few feet of empty space between the two. She would need to be swift in order to avoid being crushed beneath the whirring tread.

She paused to time the progress of the machine. It would surge forward several inches, then hold as the bore ground away, breaking up the stone. The machine seemed to hold position for twenty to thirty seconds before the bore had done sufficient work for the machine to inch forward once more.

Kasey waited as the machine lumbered forward several inches, then halted. As soon as machine came to a halt, she scrambled forward on her hands and knees. Shimmying in front of the tread, she found herself in the narrow confines between the treads themselves and the wall of the tunnel. It was barely bigger than she was.

Without warning the machine lurched forward. Kasey swung her legs to the side as the mechanical tread came crushing down barely an inch from her thigh.

Phew.

Kasey let out a slow breath.

Oh, how Henley would hate this. Not that he'd fit.

Rolling onto her back, she slid along beside the machine until she found what she was looking for: a ledge where the steel skirt of the machine disappeared, and steel steps lead up the side of the vehicle. Grabbing the lowest of the steps, she pulled herself off the ground and began to climb them. Rung by rung, she ascended, scaling the side of the tunnel borer. The steps led to a landing and the driver's cabin. Catching her breath, she clung to the side of the machine. She was almost six feet off the ground.

The machine lurched forward once more, and Kasey grabbed the ladder with both hands to avoid being thrown free from the side of the machine. To fall between the machine and the wall would likely result in being crushed to death.

When the vehicle came to a halt, Kasey stole a look in the window. The machine had no windshield, which made sense when she thought about it. There wasn't really anything but the back of the bore to look at, and it would only provide a structural weakness that falling stones might shatter. Instead, the cabin housed a complex dashboard of flashing lights and read outs designed to inform the driver of the machine's vital signs and progress.

The driver himself seemed to be in a world of his own. He rested his legs on the dashboard, his head buried in a book. A pair of earmuffs drowned out the incessant boring of the machine.

Kasey wondered if he truly understood the precariousness of his position. Did the Shinigami acolytes know what was going to happen, or were they simply following blindly, clutching at the promise of eternal life? The man was literally sitting on a bomb, clearly oblivious that his actions were about to result in the death of millions of people. Not to mention his own if the device detonated before he was able to get clear of it.

Kasey reached for the door and wrenched it open.

As he raised his head, she saw the man's lips move but with the background noise of the tunnel she couldn't hear a word he was saying. His wide-eyed expression and slackened jaw told her everything she needed to know: he'd not been expecting company.

Kasey launched herself into the cabin as the Shinigami dropped his book. He lashed out with his foot, clipping her in the ribs. She fell sideways and slammed into the dashboard. There was a lurch as the boring machine picked up power and shuddered forward. The sudden momentum caused her to roll across the dashboard, crunching buttons and levers. The same motion launched the driver into her lap.

She grabbed at the driver, pulling him against her. He drove his elbow into her stomach, but the vest took the worst of the blow and she simply gritted her teeth. Wrapping her legs around the driver, she locked him in place as she reached around his throat. Slowly, purposefully, she choked the life out of him.

Pushing off the dash, he stood up, taking Kasey with him. Turning, he threw himself backwards against the steel wall of the driver's compartment. Kasey's back bore the worst of the blow, but her head still clipped the bulkhead. Her vision swam and her legs went slack.

The driver bent forward, wrenching her off his back and over his shoulder. He slammed her into the floor of the cabin. Kasey hit the floor hard. The Shinigami loomed over her, smiling as he reached for the pistol in the holster at his waist.

Kasey kicked for all she was worth. The blow caught the weapon and sent the gun flying across the cabin. It skittered to a halt just before the open door that Kasey had entered through. The driver went after it as Kasey clambered to her feet. The

Shinigami and Kasey both raced across the tiny cabin but in her heart, she knew she'd already lost.

The Shinigami bent down and snatched up the weapon. Kasey took the next best option. As he raised the gun triumphantly and whirled to face her, she stretched out her hand.

Her whispered words of the incantation were drowned out by the noise of the machine. The fist of air struck the Shinigami in the chest like a charging bull. There was nowhere for him to go but out. The enchantment knocked him through the open door of the cabin and into the stone wall beyond it. He bounced off the stone and hit the machine, before gravity dragged him downward. His scream filled the tunnel as an almost imperceptible bounce signaled the boring machine had crushed him beneath its enormous bulk.

Kasey breathed a sigh of relief. There was no time to rest on her laurels though. The machine continued grinding forward, boring toward the fault line. Turning to the dashboard, she studied the controls.

There has to be a way to shut this thing down.

Her eyes raced over the bank of controls. Lights flashed everywhere as the machine whirred away.

A flashing red light at her left drew her attention. The label below the meter read 'Engine Temperature'. The needle bounced at the far right-hand side of the display, teetering dangerously in the red.

The machine was overheating. Not really a surprise when she considered that it had likely been operating non-stop for days. Whatever button she'd hit accidentally when she'd been thrown into the dash was evidently too much for the engine to handle.

The machine lurched forward again, faster this time. It ground forward for almost thirty seconds before halting again.

It's picking up speed. Kasey realized.

She wondered if she could use her magic to bring it to a standstill. As she thought about it, she had no idea what spell would even have such an effect.

She turned to the control panel and found a series of buttons labeled 'Bore speed'. Of its five settings, the machine was operating at its highest speed. Kasey punched the zero button and brought the bore to a halt.

With the drilling ceased, the machine was simply trying to drive forward with brute strength. There was a grinding sound as the machine threw itself at the wall in front of it, to little effect. Kasey spotted a lever that had no accompanying controls or explanation, but it did rest beside the steering mechanism. The lever was pressed right to the dashboard. Reaching for the lever, she wrenched it back toward herself. As she did, the machine ground to a halt. Beneath the lever was an ignition with a set of keys hanging out of it. She turned the keys and the tunnel borer coughed and spluttered as it shut down.

I'll take these.

She lifted the keys from the ignition and slipped them into her pocket. With the machine's progress arrested, she climbed out of the cab and onto the ledge. Seeing that the ladder beside the cab continued upward, she grabbed the rungs and began to climb. It was better than trying to fit back down between the machine and the wall.

Reaching the roof of the tunnel borer, she came face-to-face with the business end of a Glock.

Kasey raised her eyes to find Sanders staring down at her.

"Oh, Kasey, it's you." He let out a breath, lowering his gun. "You gave us a heart attack. We saw you disappear under the machine, and when the bloody body was spat out a moment ago, we feared the worst."

He offered his hand and helped her up onto the roof.

"No, fortunately that was the driver. He wasn't really ready to retire, so he needed some encouragement. It took me a while to work things out, but I finally managed to turn the damn thing off."

Sanders nodded slowly, the furrow in his brow relaxing.

As she studied Sanders, he seemed to be glittering in the faint light. Leaning forward, she wiped her hand across his brow.

He started. "What are you doing?"

She lowered her hand until it caught the light better. "I was just wondering what all this dust was."

"Oh, that," Sanders said. "When the machine surged forward a moment ago, it started spitting up clouds of this dust. It's everywhere."

She looked down at her hand and studied the dust. It was green. Emerald green.

Her breath caught in her throat.

Oh, no—we're here.

CHAPTER 13

Kasey looked down at the machine. The entire steel bulk of it was covered in the thin layer of the emerald green dust. There were footsteps where Sanders and the other ADI agents had traipsed across the machine but everywhere else was coated in the dust, including the agents themselves.

"What is it, Kasey?" Sanders asked, looking at her outstretched hand.

Kasey swallowed hard and raised her gaze to him. "We're here. We've reached the deposit. This is where Akihiro plans to detonate the weapon. We need to stop it, and we need to stop it now."

"Alright. We wanted to stop the machine first. There seems to be some kind of compartment on the back of this thing. If I had to guess, I'd say the weapon is in there," Sanders replied

"Alright, let's go. There isn't a moment to lose." She turned and raced along the top of the stationary vehicle.

At the back of the machine, two large panels had been welded shut. It appeared there was no way to open it.

"Sanders?" she called, without looking up.

He came up beside her.

Sanders pointed at the welds that ran down the side of the sealed panels. *"Grafan!"*

A brilliant lance of golden energy shot out of his outstretched finger. He moved his hand around the edges, his spell cutting through the welds as if they were paper. As he completed the circuit, two agents grabbed the handles and lifted the panels off before throwing them off the back of the boring machine. With the panels removed, Kasey found herself staring at Akihiro's weapon for the first time.

The entire space was filled with bricks of explosive. Unlike conventional C4 that came formed in bricks only eleven inches long, these had been formed into immense bricks that were two feet long and one foot wide. They had been stacked on top of each other until they filled the entire rear of the boring machine. Although it was difficult to see just how far they stretched, it was immediately apparent that Akihiro had packed the machine with enough C4 to do cataclysmic damage to the Manhattan fault line.

Unlike the device in the subbasement, the bricks had no visible detonators protruding from them. Instead, affixed in the center of the stack was a glass vessel. The vessel was a square, one foot on each side and perhaps six inches deep, with a glass lid resting atop it. The entire dish was filled with a scarlet solution. The translucent liquid sloshed about within the container as if it had a mind of its own.

"What is that?" Kasey asked, staring at the strange fluid.

It glowed as it gave off a light of its own. There was something off about it. Kasey couldn't put her finger on it, but something about it wasn't right.

Sanders held his hand over the glass vessel. Closing his eyes, he lowered his hand toward the glass lid. The vessel bore the Japanese character *shi*, meaning death. As Sanders lowered his hand, the glass vessel began to shake.

As if stung, he recoiled. "It's magic."

"Magic?" Kasey looked at him. "What do you mean magic? It's a bomb isn't it?"

"That," Sanders said, pointing to the bricks of explosive, "is a bomb, no doubt about it. But this..." He gestured toward the vessel. "This is something else entirely. It's magic, but I've never felt anything like it. The energy is all wrong."

Kasey brushed her hair back behind her ear. "How could it be magic? It's here. I thought that arcane energy was felt, not seen. It's manifestations and uses, of course I've seen those, but the very essence itself...How is it possible to contain it like this?"

She reached for the vessel. Her stomach began to churn, her heart raced as if it would explode, and her brain felt like it was on fire.

She snapped her hand away.

"What the hell?" She cried as she grabbed her head.

Sanders leaned closer and nudged the vessel gently. The liquid sloshed about reluctantly.

Kasey's gaze followed it as it lapped at the edges of the container. The color, the viscosity, Kasey knew that fluid.

"It's blood," she muttered. "That entire thing is full of blood. Why the hell is it full of blood?"

"For the same reason that you are a witch, Kasey, and Henley down there is a normal. Magic, it's in your blood. It's in all of our blood. It passes from parent to child along bloodlines, the oldest inheritance the world has ever known. It's not just blood in there. It's magic. The entire vessel is coursing with it. If I had to guess, I'd say Akihiro is using it both as a detonator and as an accelerator. The arcane energy coursing through that blood will trigger the C4 and add its strength to the blast, magnifying the explosion a hundred-fold. It won't just vaporize the serpentinite, it will devastate the bedrock beneath the city. It will level the city and everyone in it. He must have enchanted the vessel simply to be able to contain it."

"Then we need to get it the hell out of there," Kasey replied, reaching for the vessel. Ignoring the pain, she ripped the lid off it.

Energy pulsed from the container. It was as if it contained a beating heart that was pumping arcane energy into the air with every powerful pulse.

Bobbing on the surface of the sickening fluid was a thick transparent cylinder.

Inside the tightly packed cylinder was a steel cylinder, a black powder, and a digital display. The digits on the display were counting backward.

00:01:29

00:01:28

00:01:27

It's a timer.

The device wasn't remote detonated. It was on a timer. A timer that was rapidly racing to zero.

"Sanders, that's the trigger. We're out of time. It's going to blow." Without a second thought, she reached into the vessel.

"Kasey, no!" Sanders shouted, wrenching her hand away. "You can't stick your hand in there."

He lifted his pistol. With a flick of his hand, the magazine dropped free and clattered as it struck the top of the machine. Pulling back the slide, he ejected the cartridge that was in the chamber. Then, before Kasey could stop him, he lowered the barrel into the swirling broth. After two long seconds, he lifted the pistol out.

The barrel had entirely melted off. There was no trace of the steel; it had simply been absorbed into the surging energy coursing through the blood.

Sanders tossed the useless pistol off the back of the machine.

00:00:43

00:00:42

00:00:41

Kasey shook her fist in frustration. "If we don't remove that trigger, it's going to go off. That piece of steel will shatter the cylinder and whatever that black powder is will mix with the blood and detonate. We'll all die. There is no getting away from here in time. We must disarm it. How do we get the damn thing out of there if it melts everything that touches it?"

"Carefully," Sanders replied.

Reaching into the vessel, Sanders avoided touching the blood as he tried to gingerly lift the cylinder by carefully holding the flat ends of the glass trigger. Each time he touched it, it simply bobbed beneath the surface.

00:00:18

00:00:17

00:00:16

"Sanders, it's not working," Kasey said, breathing hard.

Sanders slipped, his left index finger grazing the surface of the blood. He screamed as he yanked his hand out of the solution. His finger glowed red and began to darken. Soon, the entire pad of his finger had turned pitch black.

Sanders bit down to keep himself from screaming as his finger rotted before his eyes. Tears welled up in his eyes at the pain.

"Noah!" Kasey gasped as Sanders' flesh melted off the bone.

00:00:09

00:00:08

00:00:07

"It's too late," Kasey muttered. "This can't happen."

She leaned forward and raised her hand.

There's no other way. I have to just grab the cylinder.

She locked eyes with Sanders.

He shook his head. "Kasey, no!"

00:00:06

00:00:05

00:00:04

Sanders lunged for the vessel; his fingers wrapped around the glass trigger. Ripping it out of the solution, he hurled it as far as he could.

00:00:03

00:00:02

00:00:01

The trigger struck the stone floor of the tunnel and shattered, spraying black powder everywhere.

00:00:00

The display flickered out and went dead.

Sanders dropped to his knees. His screams echoed along the tunnel as the flesh of his left hand began to darken and blister. Kasey couldn't look away. The flesh of his hand sloughed off, leaving his hand bare to the bone. He writhed in agony.

The agent standing beside Kasey doubled over and vomited over the edge of the tunneling machine.

Kasey had a much stronger stomach, but the sight of Sanders' ruined hand was making her feel queasy. Sucking in a deep breath to settle the worst of it, she crouched down beside Sanders and examined his hand. She paused. Everywhere his hand had come into contact with the solution was dissolving. The flesh was gone, and now the bones were crumbling to dust before her eyes.

"Kasey, be honest with me, how bad is it?" Sanders panted through the pain.

"I've seen worse," she replied. "You're still with us, and you're not going anywhere. Why did you have to go and do something like that, you damn fool?"

"It worked, didn't it?" Sanders replied, grinding his teeth so hard Kasey could almost feel it.

"That it did. We beat him, Sanders. You've destroyed the weapon and as soon as I make sure you don't bleed to death on me, I'm going to make him pay for all of this. Your hand, John, Arthur, the bomb, and every life he has taken to get it here. He's going to pay for everything."

"You'll have to beat Hades to it. Good luck with that," Sanders said, trying to smile between heavy pants of agony.

Kasey took hold of his arm, but he bucked in pain and cried out.

Turning to the agents, she called out, "Hold him down. We need to cauterize the wound before he bleeds out."

The surrounding agents clustered around Sanders and pinned him down by his arms and legs.

Crouching over his arm, Kasey pat him on the chest. "It'll be okay. I just need to see what we're dealing with."

He nodded, his lips pressed together in a flat line.

She examined the wound. The solution had eaten straight through his hand, leaving it as a bloody stump just above the wrist.

As she studied it, the depth of his sacrifice struck her. By reputation, Sanders was one of the greatest combat mages in the world, but in spite of everything he had traded his hand for all of their lives.

Kasey fought back a tear. He wasn't going to bleed to death in her arms. She wouldn't let him.

After tearing strips off Sanders' shirt, she gingerly wrapped the stump of his arm. The bleeding slowed, giving her the time she needed to take more lasting action.

Holding both of her hands over his ruined hand, she chanted, "Gwella!"

Her hands glowed, and a radiant golden light descended from her fingers, gently bathing Sanders' wounded arm.

Closing her eyes, she focused all of her will on the task before her. She was never gifted in the healing arts but knowing what she needed to accomplish she poured her soul into it. Her understanding of the human anatomy helped her fill in her deficiencies with the healing arts. Channeling arcane energy into Sanders to bolster his flagging reserves, she cauterized the wound, sealing the severed blood vessels, and soothed his tortured nerves.

She did her best to still her racing heart, but even as the energy flowed through her, she could feel every beat as it pounded away in a chest.

Why did you have to do that? It should have been me. Stopping the attack was my job, my mission. Don't let him pay the price for it, please.

Kasey pleaded silently as she guided her healing enchantment, pouring as much of her strength into Sanders as she could.

Closing her fist, Kasey opened her eyes. Sanders was lying dead-still against the cold steel of the machine.

She gently shook his chest. "Sanders!"

Sanders didn't move.

She checked his pulse. It was faint, but still there. Leaning down, she pressed her face close to his.

Her heart leapt as his shallow breath puffed against her cheek. *Oh, good, he's still alive.*

For a fleeting moment, she'd worried that she'd botched her healing efforts. It was more likely that the pain had finally overcome him.

She got to her feet. "It's okay. He's going to be okay." Her voice was shaky, and she hoped that she sounded a lot more confident than she felt. "Now that we've stopped the device, we need to get him back to the surface. He's weak but he'll live. He's in no condition to walk so, Henley, you're up. You can ditch the backpack. It's no good to us now. You'll have more precious cargo."

Henley nodded and reached up, waving for Kasey and the agents to pass Sanders down.

Together, they gingerly lowered Sanders off the back of the boring machine and onto Henley's shoulder. It was a less than glamorous mode of transportation but there was no other choice. Sanders wasn't going to be walking out of the tunnel on his own and Kasey had no intention of leaving him behind.

Kasey turned to the remaining agents. "Alright, with Sanders down, I'm going to need you to follow my lead. You two, stick with Henley. Don't stop till you reach the outer police cordon. When you get there, requisition a car and take him straight to the Administorum. Don't let anyone get in your way. If you encounter any resistance, put it down, with extreme prejudice."

One of the agents nodded. "Sure, Chase. No worries, you can count on us."

"Alright, Henley, take it away, but go easy with him," she said. "He matters more than you know."

Henley raised an eyebrow at her.

"He's the most important wizard in my world. He heads the Arcane Council. Your world and mine are still coming to terms. There will be conflict, and we're going to need a leader who can help us negotiate these trying times. Sanders is the man we need in charge, and for that to happen, he needs to survive today. You hold on your shoulders our hope for peace and prosperity. Nothing else matters, do you understand?"

"No pressure," Henley replied. "I'll get him there."

He turned and, with Sanders on his back, began working his way back up the tunnel, flanked on either side by agents of the ADI.

Kasey watched them a moment, then shook her head. "Okay, now that Sanders is safe, I need four of you to stay behind and render this weapon inoperable. There is still enough C4 to do irreparable damage. We need to separate it from the device. Sanders may have prevented the trigger from detonating, but this tunnel is far from stable. We need to ensure that the C4 and the blood never come in contact with each other. Do you understand me?"

The agents nodded.

"You saw just how dangerous that solution is. Don't touch it, under any circumstance. I just need you to remain behind and remove the C4. Take turns and ferry it back up the tunnel, away from the fault line. I know it'll take time, but it's important. We can't leave it undetonated by the fault line. Take it in shifts, one block at a time, and get it back to the subbasement. The technician from the bomb squad is still there, he'll ensure that it is disposed of."

"What do you want us to do with the blood?" the sandy haired ADI agent asked.

Kasey looked at the scarlet liquid swirling about in the glass containment chamber. "That vessel isn't going anywhere. It's bolted down, and besides it's too dangerous. As soon as you've emptied the C4, put the doors back on the chamber and seal it permanently. We'll deal with it later, or we'll bring the tunnel down on top of it. Either way, we can't risk it falling into the wrong hands. The rest of you, we're heading for the surface. We may have stopped the device, but the architect of this madness is still on the loose. Akihiro needs to pay for all of this."

She climbed down off the tunnel boring machine and dusted herself off. Leaving the four agents to deal with the explosives, she counted those at her side. Of the contingent that she and Sanders had led down into the catacombs, only a dozen remained.

She hoped it would be enough.

She took a deep breath. "Agents, let's move out."

The agents followed her as she led the charge back toward the surface. Any moment now, Akihiro would realize the device had failed to detonate. When he did, there would be hell to pay.

As she moved, Kasey wondered how the Master of the Shinigami would respond. Would he make a run for it? Somehow, she doubted it.

The Master may have fled the council chambers when his identity had been revealed, but that had been when his plot was still viable, and he'd carved a bloody path through the chambers on his way out. He was relentless. With his plot ruined, there was every chance he was on his way to the weapon right now.

"Keep your eyes open, everyone," she called. "If Akihiro doesn't run for his life, he'll be gunning for us. We need to be ready."

They reached the site of the Shinigami ambush. There were dozens of bodies. In her haste to find the weapon, Kasey hadn't even realized how many agents they had lost.

Good agents.

She picked her way through the carnage. They deserved better, but it would have to wait.

"Chase, I think this one's still kicking."

Kasey turned to find a wiry young agent in his thirties, with a shaggy mop of brown hair, nudging one of the Shinigami acolytes with his foot.

The body stirred, its hand reaching out as it struggled to rise.

Kasey walked over and looked down at the wounded acolyte. Raising her gaze, she caught the agent's eye. "Then put him down. Only a few minutes ago, they were trying to slit our throats. If you let him back up, he's only going to try again."

The agent scrunched up his face. "Put him down?"

"With a bullet," Kasey replied. "And be quick about it."

"Execute him?" the agent replied. "I can't do that."

"Oh, don't give me that. It's only been a matter of days since the Arcane Council was ready to kill me, and for a hell of a lot less," Kasey said. Pointing furiously at the fallen agents, she continued. "These are a dozen of your comrades, lying here, in this hellhole because of him and his kind. How are you going to feel if one of them kills the agents we've left behind to disarm the weapon, or worse yet, triggers the weapon themselves? Put a bullet in him, or give me the gun and I'll do it. Either way, we have no more time to waste."

"When you put it like that..." the agent replied. He raised his pistol and fired twice. The Shinigami bucked as the bullets struck him before collapsing in the dirt.

Kasey patted the agent on the back.

"Glad we're on the same page." Stepping over the body, she continued up the path. Pausing, she looked over her shoulder. "While you're at it, put one in all of them, just to be safe. No half measures."

Gunfire rang through the tunnel, as Kasey continued her upward march toward the basement.

CHAPTER 14

C learing the basement, Kasey raced up the stairs. She could feel the fatigue starting to burn in her legs, but she pushed on. Until Akihiro was caught, there could be no rest. The Master of the Shinigami would not simply quit, and right now the entire strike force was in peril. "Chase, we have some movement here on the ground floor. The elevator is on the move," a voice crackled through the comms.

"Roger that. We're on our way right now," Kasey replied, as she leaned over the rail and looked up toward the surface. There were only a few flights left to go. "We'll be there in less than a minute."

She bounded up the stairs as quickly as she could force her legs to carry her. Footsteps behind and below her in the stairwell told her that the ADI was doing its best to keep up.

Her comm came to life again. "Bishop, here. Kasey, I've got movement here too. I'm looking at Park Avenue. It seems every sixth floor is a maintenance floor. They're open to the elements to reduce sway. It should be empty and sealed but we can see movement up there. Someone is up there. What's more, they have the advantage of height. We can't stay here. We'll be pinned down and exposed. It will be like shooting fish in a barrel."

"Roger that, Bishop. Go to ground and keep your eyes peeled. We've defused the device, but Akihiro is going to be on the move. I doubt he'll give up so easily. Ground floor, be ready to give him hell. He can't be allowed to leave the building."

"Too late, Kasey," the agent on the ground floor replied. "I think he's here."

Kasey's heart skipped a beat, her hand shaking as she gripped the rail and pulled herself upward. "I'm almost there." She panted, racing up the final set of stairs and onto the landing.

As she reached the ground floor, the elevator doors opened, and Akihiro stepped out.

The Master of the Shinigami did not bother with any illusion now. He was dressed in a simple silk robe that was cinched with a simple obi. His jet-black hair was drawn back into a top knot. At his waist hung the blade that he had used to kill both John and Arthur Ainsley. Compared to the heavily armed strike force lying in wait, he looked positively defenseless.

Looks can be deceiving, Kasey reminded herself.

The look on his face made Kasey's hands shake. His thin lips were drawn, his dark eyes narrowed on the strike force before him. His chest heaved slowly with each breath. His barely contained rage was palpable. Around his neck dangled the same medallion she'd seen in the Arcane Council chambers. The personal shield enchantment had allowed him to walk unscathed through a storm of fire. The amulet radiated a sickly green glow; it appeared its energy had been replenished since the skirmish in the Council Chambers.

Kasey shouted, "Fire!"

The strike force of assembled agents, Helldrakes, and police officers opened fire on the elevator. The noise was deafening as dozens of submachine guns and assault rifles poured a withering storm of lead at the Master of the Shinigami. He raised his hand and the ward at his chest glowed the same haunting emerald hue as when he had drained the life out of John Ainsley.

Hundreds of bullets pounded into the protective barrier, but the shield stopped them dead in their tracks. The only sign of any impact was the disheartening pitter patter of the lead striking the ground as they dropped harmlessly to the floor. The pile of lead grew steadily, but Akihiro stood unfazed.

What's his plan? Why isn't he attacking?

The fusillade weakened as the strike force began to run dry. The furious din grew still as spent magazines were ejected and discarded.

"Keep it up. No shield can last forever," Kasey shouted. "As soon as it runs out, he's a dead man."

Akihiro turned until he was facing the stairwell. His eyes glimmered as they locked on Kasey.

"Oh, Miss Chase, you are as persistent as you are irritating," he said. "I'll give you that. Losing John wasn't enough for you? Haven't you had enough? I spared your life in the Underpass. You should have taken it and run. Instead, you've thrown it away. You are a foolish little girl."

Kasey's hands shook with rage. "Let me live? You ran for your life, you coward. Now your device is destroyed, and your plan is ruined. All of that planning, all of the time you spent masquerading as Arthur Ainsley, what have you got to show for it? The city is safe and so is everyone in it. So, you can kiss your immortality goodbye."

Akihiro bared his teeth. "Ever the optimist, Miss Chase, you don't have what it takes to understand the forces at work against you. For centuries, wizards have been forced to live in the shadows pretending we don't exist. All so these insecure insects we are unfortunate enough to share a world with don't get trigger-happy and decide to try and slaughter us again. Is that all you think this is about? Simply killing a few normals?

"True, the weapon might bring us immortality, but it will also grant us enough power to ensure no one would ever be able to withstand us. In one swift motion, it would destroy this city, the financial heart of this country, and plunge it into chaos and anarchy. Think of it—the world's greatest superpower brought to its knees in a single day. The normals will be too busy quarreling among themselves to fight back. Now you've given them hope and turned on your own kind. It's only a matter of time before they move against us.

"You have made the coming war all the more difficult and yet you gloat. With the power we gained here, we would have been unstoppable. There would be no more hiding, no more running, no more cowering in the shadows. We would be what we are always meant to be—gods among men to be revered, not hunted. In your foolish idealism, you've brought peril on us all. Just wait until it's you and your family being hunted. You will feel differently then."

"But there are wizards here too," Kasey replied. "The attack would have slaughtered them all. It would have wiped out the entire Arcane Council."

Akihiro shrugged. "All the better. The council is made up of simpering fools who don't possess the backbone or stomach to do what is truly required. They are of little use to me anyway. We will not cower in the shadows a moment longer."

"Well, I'm delighted to disappoint you. Your weapon seems to be experiencing a little technical difficulty. It won't be going off today, or any other for that matter."

Akihiro bit his lip.

Kasey pressed her advantage. "That's right, we found the weapon, and now it's in pieces. Good luck bringing the city to the ground without it. You'll have to do it one building at a time like a normal terrorist."

Akihiro shook his head. "How could you have found the weapon? You only just arrived."

"It helps when you know exactly where to look. You don't get it, do you? I saw it, over and over and over. The first time I witnessed what you had in store for the city, I was twelve. Ever since, my whole life has been spent preparing for today, and every time you sent a new body to the morgue to advance your murderous plot, you put them in my path. The visions they granted led us straight to your weapon. How does it feel to know that years before you laid the foundations of this murderous plot, fate was already conspiring to thwart it? You're beat. Give it up already."

Akihiro folded his arms. "You mistake delay for defeat. Do you really think this paltry show of strength is enough to defy me? I will lay waste to you all. In death you will serve a far greater purpose than you have in life."

"Your threats are empty, Akihiro. Your strength wanes, your forces have been routed. You too will fall. It ends here and now."

"On the contrary, Kasey. I am stronger than I've ever been. You, on the other hand, are looking utterly spent. Tell me, how much of that blood is yours? Do you truly believe you could stand against me, even if you wanted to? And tell me, where is Sanders? I was hoping to finish what I started in the Underpass. His absence is telling, but then fear will do that."

"Afraid of you? In your dreams. It was Sanders that destroyed your weapon," Kasey spat back.

Akihiro smiled. "Oh, did he now? Ah, Sanders, always the hero. What price did he pay for that? Did it kill him?"

"He'll live," Kasey replied, not wanting to give him the satisfaction of knowing Sanders had lost a hand.

"It hardly matters. The fool was your only hope. Now he convalesces when you need him the most. A few agents, a handful of police, and a battered little girl don't stand a chance."

"Take another step and I'll kick your ancient ass. You might be a zillion years old, but I can see the future, Akihiro, and you're not in it."

Akihiro scoffed. "Nice try, but your bluff is hollow. You see, Miss Chase, you might fancy yourself a hero, but not everyone is as willing to die for a losing cause as you are." Turning, he addressed the strike force gathered before him. "You have all been lied to. I am not your enemy. I am your ally. You've come here today to destroy me at the behest of this deluded child and a council of fools. But know this, those who side with me will join us as we partake of immortality and rule this world until the end of time. Join me now. It's not too late."

Hades hollered back, "Join you? You slaughtered a dozen of my men for sport. What's more, you made a spectacle of it on TV. You butchered them for the whole world to see. You speak of a war against the normals. You are the cause of that conflict. Until a week ago, they were ignorant of our very existence, but you outed our entire society just to buy time for this madness. Your words cannot to be trusted."

Hades stood with both pistols in hand, trained on the elevator. The Lord of the Underworld wasn't going to give the Master of the Shinigami a single inch of ground.

Akihiro glowered. "On the contrary, Hades—or should I say, Angelo. Yes, I know your true name. I know exactly who you are. I know where you live, holed up in that little cesspit of a club. You lord over the other miscreants in this city like you matter. Your half-baked criminal empire doesn't hold a candle to the Brotherhood."

Brotherhood? It was the same title Arthur Ainsley had used right before he'd been stabbed to death by Akihiro in the confessional. It seemed that both Arthur and Akihiro were counted among its ranks.

Who was this Brotherhood?

"The Brotherhood began centuries before you were even conceived. You are mere infants playing at a game you do not truly understand. Besides, we would never deign to throw in our lot with the Arcane Council. It's offensive. Some criminal overlord you are. You're Sanders' lackey. You know it, your men know it. How long do you think they will tolerate this dalliance with the law?"

Hades' face flushed red and he squeezed the trigger. The Desert Eagle in his right hand bucked as it fired. Akihiro's shield flared as the bullet struck it.

Akihiro waggled his finger. "Come now, Hades, don't be like that. You'll force my hand. You should know, I didn't kill your men for sport. There were plenty of other targets that would have suited my purposes. Unfortunately, they ambushed me much like you are now and I gave them the same choice that I will give you. Join with me and forsake this foolish effort or die. If you join me, we will live forever. If you don't, you'll die here and now.

Hades spat on the floor. "Never. You may bluff and bluster but you're not leaving here alive. If you had half a chance, you wouldn't be stalling. You'd have killed us already."

Akihiro shrugged. "Well, you can't say I didn't try. I gave you every chance to change your mind. Still, you can't see what is right in front of you. Life, salvation, immortality."

"You're insane," Hades replied. "Too much life has made you mad. Your dabbling in necromancy has driven you to delusion."

Akihiro sighed as he crossed his arms. "Oh, no, Hades, on the contrary, it's made me see things more clearly, something you are unwilling or unable to do. Zryx, how about you? Tell me, are you seeing things more clearly now? I told you he was weak. Don't you see, he's just another pawn of the council."

Hades whirled as Zryx racked her submachine gun. Menace gleamed in her eyes. It was the look she'd had when she'd insisted Kasey be thrown into the ring against Dozer. Her eyes were a glinting mixture of madness and murder.

"I accept," Zryx answered.

"No!" Kasey shouted as Zryx raised the gun and squeezed the trigger.

Hades buckled as the submachine gun rounds caught him in the chest.

He collapsed, his face a twisted grimace of shock and betrayal.

As Hades fell, Zryx shouted, "Hell is under new management. Any of you that want to join your old boss, raise your hand. Any of you that are with me, let's go. Kill these sycophants and weaklings now!"

The Helldrakes fell in behind Zryx without hesitation.

Kasey's heart stopped as the magnitude of Zryx's betrayal struck her. Of the strike force they had assembled to stop

Akihiro, only forty odd fighters remained. Now a full third of them, the Helldrakes, had turned on the police and ADI at point-blank range. The result would be catastrophic.

As the strike force returned fire, the lobby descended into madness.

CHAPTER 15

Kasey shook as she watched the Helldrakes turn on their former allies with brutal efficiency. In such close proximity, Hades' heavily armed shock troops were unavoidable.

Despite being caught flat-footed, the ADI responded with a tenacity born of desperation. With no room to maneuver, the ADI resolutely held their ground, firing back with precision, picking off the aggressive Helldrakes.

One of Hades' wizards, bellowing in the ancient tongue, unleashed a fireball that crashed into an ADI contingent clustered behind a pallet of tiles. The swirling inferno washed over the barrier. A piercing shout told Kasey that one of the agents had been caught in the inferno.

The Helldrakes spellcaster cackled with glee at the devastation, but his gloating was cut short as the ADI found him. The wizard's mouth had barely closed when his eyes went wide with shock, milliseconds before his brains were blown out the back of his skull.

A rotund and balding agent, crouched just inside the doorway, had dropped the gloating wizard with a single bullet to the head.

The brunette agent beside Kasey sank to the floor. Clutching at her stomach, she struggled to stem the blood flow. Kasey bent down to help her, but without her med kit, there was little she could do to help. Using her magic to heal a single agent in the midst of the unfolding carnage was like trying to hold back a river with a handkerchief. If they didn't win, they were all dead anyway. She waved Kasey away and with her back against the wall, she used her other hand to fire back at the traitorous Helldrakes.

In the midst of the chaos, Akihiro stood still, protected by the safety of his amulet. He smiled as he bathed in the chaos of the conflict surrounding him.

As the Helldrakes and agents continued to battle, the Master of the Shinigami began to chant. The haunting monotone Japanese was unnerving, but for all his conjuring, it seemed to have no influence on the chaos around him.

Then Kasey saw it.

An emerald wisp of smoke rose from the fallen ADI agent before her. It floated across the chamber to where Akihiro stood chanting.

He's harvesting their life force.

As the bodies continued to drop, the wisps became a veritable river of energy flowing into him.

"Stop!" Kasey shouted. "You're only making him stronger. Don't you see?"

No one seemed to hear her.

There's no stopping them now, but even killing the Helldrakes will strengthen Akihiro.

It was a deadly conundrum.

Zryx loped giddily through the chamber, her submachine gun chattering madly as she took shots at anything that moved. The Helldrakes occupied one flank, utilizing tile pallets and the support pillars in the lobby to protect themselves while coordinating fire against the superior number of ADI agents and police officers.

The resolute remnants of the task force were desperately falling back to the cover afforded by the pallets separating Kasey from Akihiro and the Helldrakes.

The lobby itself was so densely packed that it was no better than a gun fight in an alleyway. Both sides were stuck squaring off at point-blank range. One wrong move would see them fall.

One of the ADI combat mages launched a ruby red lance of pure energy across the chamber, shearing straight through a Helldrake, separating his torso from his legs as it carved him in half at the waist.

A pair of Helldrakes worked their way up the right flank. The combat mage shifted targets. As his focus shifted, so did the lance. The Helldrakes ducked for cover behind a support pillar.

The arcane lance followed them like a dog with a bone, carving into the pillar. Masonry blasted out from the pillar as the energy carved gaping holes through it. The mage doubled down, tearing into the pillar in an effort to reach the Helldrakes sheltering behind it.

Kasey raced for the cover afforded by the pallets. "Hey, easy there," she shouted over the fray. "You'll bring down the building and kill us all."

The ADI agent paused, then ceased his casting and dropped back behind cover. Using magic in the tight confines of the lobby without further compromising the damaged structure was a careful balancing act. One overzealous enchantment would bring the entire building down, and there was nothing to be gained from mutually assured destruction.

Kasey peered over the edge of the tile pallet. Three Helldrakes moved down the left flank, using the cover of the shattered elevator shafts to surprise the ADI.

Kasey knew she had to ignore her own advice and deal with them before they began firing at the ADI's exposed flank.

Channeling her might, she let her power flow through her. "Mellt!".

The bolt of lightning leapt across the room in a heartbeat. It crackled as it split through the air. With unyielding power, the lightning plunged straight for the elevator. In the dense confines of ruined elevator shaft there was no way it could miss.

The savage strike hammered into the three Helldrakes, energy coursing through their bodies, overloading their hearts before grounding itself into the floor. Smoke rose from their armored torsos as they dropped.

They won't be getting back up.

At her right, another ADI agent fell as a series of gunshot wounds stitched across his chest, before punching through his neck. As Kasey traced the trajectory of the threat, she saw Zryx with her submachine gun raised.

Kasey's blood boiled. There was nothing she hated more than a traitor. Someone who was willing to turn on their own kind and shoot them in the back was the lowest form of scum. Hades' fall had been unexpected, but it would not go unavenged.

Zryx met Kasey's stare and bared her teeth in an angry snarl. She raised her weapon.

Kasey had other ideas. *"I Gymryd Ar Wahan."*

Zryx jammed down on the trigger, grinning like a maniac.

Kasey dropped down, seeking the shelter afforded by the timber. She heard the bullets slam into the pallet, but then the gun clicked empty, followed by a clattering sound. Peeking over the edge, Kasey couldn't help but smile at the confused look on Zryx's face.

Her gun was falling to the floor, piece by piece.

Kasey had taken that spell from Sanders' extensive repertoire.

"No!" Zryx shouted fighting to keep the weapon in one piece. Her efforts were in vain as the barrel came loose, falling uselessly to the floor.

She hurled the remaining pieces of the disassembling weapon straight at Kasey. Kasey ducked under the weapon, before leaping the pallet and charging straight at the traitor.

As Zryx growled and ran toward her, Kasey dropped her shoulder. She crash-tackled the treacherous woman to the tile floor. Together they went down, tussling across the tile. Kasey wrestled her way on top as Zryx kicked Kasey in the groin before clawing at her neck.

Batting away Zryx's arms, Kasey slammed her head into the tiles. She closed one fist around the Zryx's throat. Zryx thrashed wildly seeking to throw Kasey free. Steadying herself, Kasey drew back and drove her right fist straight into Zryx's face. Zryx snarled, barring her teeth. Kasey's follow up shattered her nose. As blood poured from Zryx's face, Kasey felt tremendous satisfaction.

From the moment she had met Hades' insane accomplice, she had disliked her. The feeling had been mutual with Zryx doing everything she could to ensure Kasey died in the ring with Dozer. Turning on Hades was the last straw.

Kasey wrestled with Zryx who used both her legs as leverage to launch free. She reached for her belt.

Kasey felt more than saw the danger as Zryx lunged at her with a knife. She rolled away from wicked looking barbed edge. The blade sliced against the Kevlar of her vest and she was grateful for its presence. As Zryx lunged again, Kasey seized her wrist. She twisted it sharply, seeking to wrench the knife from her grip.

Zryx raised her second hand and clutched her own wrist. Using both arms, she lifted the blade and tried to drive the weapon forward, aiming for the exposed flesh above Kasey's vest. As the blade teetered closer, Kasey shoved back. Zryx inched the knife closer. Clutching Zryx's hands in hers, Kasey wrenched her forward and drove her head into Zryx's already broken nose.

Zryx howled in pain. Kasey seized the opportunity to go for the knife. Zryx launched forward, slamming into Kasey.

As Kasey fell backwards, she grabbed at the knife. She landed on her back. Zryx followed her down, straddling her stomach, both hands lodged on the blade, trying to drive it through Kasey.

Using all of her strength, Kasey wrestled the blade to the side and It slammed into the floor only inches from her left ear. Zryx tried to yank the blade free, but Kasey held firm. To lose the knife would be her death. Zryx leaned down and bit Kasey just above the wrist.

"Ow," Kasey gasped, letting go of the knife.

She couldn't believe Zryx had just bit her. Her heart stopped as Zryx yanked the blade away and held it aloft, grinning madly.

With both hands on the knife, she raised it over Kasey's chest. "Goodbye, my dear Jenny."

"Go to hell!" Kasey replied, raising her hands.

The gesture caught Zryx off guard, and she cocked her head to the side.

"*Pêl Tân.*" Kasey barked as she flipped her palms up.

Zryx's eyes went wide as Kasey's hands began to glow.

Kasey felt the energy flow through her being as fire streamed from both palms, straight toward Zryx sitting atop her. Zryx screamed as the flames consumed her from the waist up. The knife fell uselessly from her hands as she clutched at her flaming face. Grabbing Zryx by the belt, Kasey hurled the toasted corpse off her and onto the floor.

The Helldrakes faltered and dove for cover. Hades and Zryx were dead. Having turned on the strike force, the Helldrakes had signed their own death warrants.

With Zryx's body still a smoking wreck on the floor, they looked to Kasey and the ADI. Sharing glances with each other they looked to their only remaining ally—the same being who had promised them immortality: Akihiro.

Kasey's heart sank as she realized the Master of the Shinigami was on the move again.

Akihiro, flanked by three of his disciples, was making a break for the front door. Clearly the Shinigami had no intention of reigniting the weapon; he'd simply baited the Helldrakes into distracting the strike force so that he could flee undetected.

"Get him," Kasey shouted at the strike force. "We can't let him leave."

She raced after Akihiro. One of the few remaining Helldrakes moved to block her path.

Without slowing down, Kasey shouted, "*Dwrn Ygwynt!*"

The spell struck the Helldrake with such force, it blew him clear through the window and onto the sidewalk beyond.

A burst of gunfire from across the room forced her to dart behind a pillar. The ADI agents traded shots with Helldrakes huddled together in a fortified position by the door. Three Helldrakes hiding behind a cluster of pallets was all that stood between her and the retreating Akihiro.

"Bishop, are you there?" she said into her comm. "Akihiro is leaving. We need to take him down now."

"We're trying, Kasey but we are under siege as well," Bishop said, breathless. "There are snipers on the sixth floor. We've lost two officers already and we've had to go to ground."

High caliber shots punctured the background of the communication. Suddenly it sunk in: the motion that Bishop had spotted earlier had been Akihiro's supporters getting into position. They knew the Master was making his way to the street and they were providing overwatch. The acolytes were trading their own lives and freedom in an attempt to allow Akihiro to escape.

Kasey couldn't let that happen.

"He's on the street," she said. "Do you have a shot, Bishop?"

"Negative. We're pinned down in the retail tower. Don't worry, West is tightening the cordon as we speak. We'll get him."

Kasey shook her head. She couldn't leave this to the precincts. What chance did police officers stand against the Master of the Shinigami? She'd just watched him shrug off dozens of bullets with no effect. The amulet he wore was proving to be potent protection against the mundane weapons. She had hoped that the sheer weight of fire they had dedicated to it would have drained it of energy, but her hope was in vain.

She watched as Akihiro and his men raced toward their freedom.

No, no, no, it doesn't end like this.

She had watched Akihiro get away time and time again. Every time he slipped through their fingers, it cost countless lives. After everything he had done, Kasey couldn't countenance him slipping away quietly into the setting sun.

"Cover me," Kasey shouted.

The ADI agents rose as one, pouring firepower into the Helldrakes' positions. The Helldrakes retreated behind the safety of the pallets.

Kasey emerged from behind the pillar. As she raced for the door, she kept her eyes locked on the entrenched position. If one of the Helldrakes raised his head, he would realize how open she was. If they got off even one shot, there would be no missing her.

She sprinted for the door, hoping to be past the Helldrakes before they realized what had happened.

A Helldrake peered over the top of the pallet.

No such luck.

He raised his weapon and drew a bead on her.

"Chwyth Dinistriol!" she chanted.

Her spell hit the pallet barrier like a cruise missile. As it detonated, it shattered the tiles, the pallets, and everything within ten feet. The shock wave from the spell rolled through the ground floor lobby, knocking Kasey to the ground. The building itself shook as the blast rocked the structure.

Oh, no, that's done it.

As Kasey slid across the floor, her heart raced. She had forgotten about the broken pillar.

Her back slammed into a wall. She waited.

As the building settled, she let herself breathe again.

Pushing to her feet, she looked at the Helldrakes' position. It had been annihilated. Where there had been pallets and enemies only moments earlier, there was now only a smoking crater. Shards of tile were scattered everywhere while a dust cloud lingered overhead. Of the Helldrakes there was no evidence that they had ever been there. Kasey's spell had obliterated them.

With no time to revel in her victory, she ran for the door.

CHAPTER 16

Bursting through the front door, Kasey found herself back on the sidewalk. The street had darkened as sunset rapidly approached. Flanked by his acolytes, Akihiro made his way onto the street, weaving between the scattered debris of the ruined helicopters.

Gunshots split the air. Kasey whipped her head to the left, tracking their source. Bishop and a small platoon of officers from the Ninth Precinct were sheltered in the ground floor of the retail building.

The first Shinigami acolyte fell, dead. Chanting, the second acolyte began to raise a ward. Before the shield finished forming, a lucky bullet took him in his thigh. The acolyte groaned as he collapsed, his shield dissipating as his concentration broke.

The third acolyte leapt for cover behind Akihiro, the Shinigami Master's amulet still proving effective against the hail of lead.

"Master!" the wounded acolyte groaned, reaching for Akihiro.

Akihiro looked at his fallen disciple, and then at the police officers pushing toward him. With a dismissive shrug, he turned his back on his fallen acolyte.

"Help me," the acolyte howled, but the plea fell on deaf ears.

As the strike force followed Kasey forward, they continued firing. The next round caught the fallen acolyte in the chest, and he went still, lying on the asphalt.

Akihiro continued to make his way to the nearest Bearcat. To him, the presence of the NYPD seemed to matter little. Shielded from their weapons by arcane means, he dismissed them as one might a bothersome fly.

"He's making a run for it," Kasey shouted. "Don't let him get that thing started."

Akihiro disappeared inside the cab of the Bearcat, only to re-emerge a moment later red-faced. He slammed the door.

The Ninth Precinct continued to pour fire onto him.

He whirled around to face them. His chest rose and fell as he shook with fury, his nonchalant demeanor shattered.

"*Shi No Honou!*" he chanted as he swung his arm like a baseball pitcher throwing out his first pitch, heaving a sphere of emerald flames at the retail precinct.

Kasey's heart stopped as the sphere of flames crossed the street and slammed into the retail center, shattering its remaining display windows.

Bishop was in there.

She started to run toward the building when Bishop threw herself clear. She hit the sidewalk and rolled as the police scattered.

Kasey skidded to a halt, relief flooding through her.

The flames erupted. One of the officers was struck, his body turning to ash at the flame's lethal caress.

Turning his attention back to making his escape, Akihiro ran for the second armored transport.

Kasey raced after him.

Akihiro climbed up into the open cab of the vehicle, and his jubilant smile told Kasey all she needed to know: he'd found a set of keys.

He turned the key and the Bearcat's engine rumbled to life. The Shinigami's last acolyte began climbing up to join his master, but Kasey had other plans for them both.

Raising her hands, she chanted, *"Maes Heulwen!"*

At her command, a sphere of blinding golden light hurtled at the armored car. It was a tamer version of the spell Sanders liked to employ. While she didn't have enough confidence in her control to turn herself into the missile, she expected it would do its work regardless. The armored vehicles had not been built to withstand an arcane assault. She hoped it would prove more than a match for the Bearcat and its occupant.

As the sphere of light hurtled toward the vehicle, Akihiro grabbed his acolyte by his shirt and launched him out of the cab. The airborne acolyte collided with Kasey's spell and was utterly obliterated, vanishing in a flash of ash and smoke.

The attack was neutralized. Kasey blinked, trying to process what had just happened.

Akihiro swept his hand before him and chanted, *"Shi No Kabe."*

The oily emerald flames streamed through the air in torrents like an arcane flamethrower. The flames fanned out from the Bearcat in a deadly wave. As the fire rolled toward her, Kasey dove forward, throwing herself behind a raised stone garden bed. Wincing as the concrete grazed her palms, she rolled until she lay flat against the granite. She waited as the emerald flames passed overhead. They were close, unsettlingly so. With every breath, she could smell the sulfurous fury of the blaze.

The energy Akihiro was expending was incredible. Kasey wondered how he managed to control and sustain his arcane reserves for such a prolonged period. The energy drain of his amulet alone should have depleted his strength but still he seemed to wield an almost limitless arcane might.

How can I compete with that?

Kasey was physically and mentally exhausted. She hurt all over and she could feel her spells weakening with each subsequent effort. Without rest, her magic would continue to wane. In the face of Akihiro's limitless power, she was beginning to feel futile.

As the flames continued to billow overhead, she remembered Sanders' comments about necromancy. And Kasey could see his meaning. There was something inherently wrong about the energy Akihiro was unleashing. It wasn't magic as she had become accustomed to; it felt tainted. The very energy leaking from his every spell seemed offensive to her, as if it had become corrupted.

Then it dawned on her. Akihiro seem to be perverting the natural order of magic, tainting each spell with the spent life force he extracted from his victims. Everything about it was alien and offensive, but Kasey suddenly understood why he never seemed to tire. He wasn't simply using the life force to prolong his life and stave off death; he was using the energy to augment his magical reserves. Drawing on them instead of the arcane, he was able to unleash far more power than an ordinary wizard.

Somehow, he was storing and using the unspent life force he had harvested. His deception in the lobby had simply been to spark more conflict so that he might harvest the dying strength of those who expired. All of a sudden, Kasey realized why they had faced less resistance than she had expected. Sanders had reported dozens of wizards defecting to Akihiro's cause and yet they had only faced a handful since arriving.

Akihiro had likely lured them to Park Avenue, simply to kill them and harvest their life force. After all, why would he wish to share his power with so many others? Those wizards that had defected hadn't remained in his employ. They'd simply been sacrificed to fuel the Shinigami's seemingly boundless lust for power. It was their energy that fueled his amulet's barrier, and the same energy that he unleashed every time he dabbled with his foul magic.

In her mind's eye, she saw the glowing amulet that had rested around his neck.

It's the key. It has to be.

She'd seen that same eerie glow many times. It glowed every time Akihiro used his magic. It pulsed whenever his shield was struck. Every time energy was exerted, the amulet responded.

The amulet was not simply a shield—it was capable of storing the fading energy of a human soul.

As the flames subsided, Kasey rose to her feet, careful to avoid any lingering wisps that danced along the sidewalk before burning out. Akihiro slammed the door of the Bearcat shut and stomped on the gas. More gunshots slammed into the armored car, but the vehicle was more than a match for the small caliber rounds. As the vehicle launched forward, Kasey took the only option available to her.

She ran for the closest Bearcat, hoping against hope that the driver hadn't taken the keys with him. She threw open the driver's door and climbed into the seat. Her gaze swept over the interior and landed on keys still dangling in the ignition. Letting out a sigh of relief, she closed the door and then twisted the keys. The Bearcat's engine spluttered into life.

As the passenger door opened, Kasey whirled, raising her right hand. She began to chant an arcane deterrent.

"Easy, Kasey, it's me," Bishop said, pausing.

Kasey clenched her fist and extinguished her spell before it manifest.

Bishop climbed inside. Her hair was mussed, she was covered in dust and bleeding from a shallow cut on her cheek.

"I can't let him get away," Kasey said, gripping the wheel. "This has to end here."

"No argument from me," Bishop replied. "I sure as hell wasn't going to let you go it alone. I've got your back. It's high time we got some payback for the Ninth Precinct."

Kasey nodded, slid the vehicle into gear, and stomped on the gas. Akihiro and the Shinigami had been responsible for decimating the Ninth Precinct and killing John. Now Sanders was wounded, and dozens of others had perished trying to halt his deadly plot.

Up ahead, Akihiro was pulling away from them.

"Oh, no, you don't," Kasey muttered, pushing the gas pedal to the floor.

The Bearcat launched forward, surprisingly responsive for such a heavy vehicle. She had never driven anything near this size, but she steered the lumbering vehicle through the debris and into the street, only to find her path blocked by the broken tail rotors of the helicopter.

There was no stopping, though. Kasey plowed straight into the debris. The steel buckled as the Bearcat ground straight over the top of it. Kasey bounced in her seat but clutched the wheel tightly.

As the impact jostled her about, Kasey thought better of her haste and shouted to Bishop, "Grab the wheel for a second."

Bishop obliged and Kasey reached for her seatbelt. Pulling it across her body, she fastened it. "Can't be too careful now."

Bishop nodded, and as Kasey took the wheel back, she reached for her own. "On second thought, if you're driving, I'd better buckle up too."

"Hey, what's that supposed to mean?" Kasey threw Bishop a sideways glare.

Bishop pointed her thumb over her shoulder. "You've only been behind the wheel for thirty seconds and you've wiped out a helicopter. I'm beginning to think there is a reason I do all the driving."

Kasey raised an eyebrow. "I guess we're about to find out."

The armored vehicle rolled past the shattered remains of the retail tower. It had definitely seen better days.

Up ahead, Akihiro's Bearcat careened straight through the intersection of East 56th Street and Park Avenue without a care in the world. If it wasn't for the police cordon having cleared the streets, he would have annihilated several lanes of traffic.

Not that he would have cared.

Kasey followed him into the intersection. With her foot to the floor, she chased him down East 56th Street. Along both sides of the street, stone and marble and glass facades rose skyward, as ground floor shops gave way to towering residential complexes. Cars lined the street, narrowing the street to little more than a single lane of traffic. As they barreled past the Renaissance hotel, a taxi tried to pull out in front of Akihiro.

Akihiro's vehicle slammed straight into the yellow cab. The taxi crumpled before being sent spinning across the sidewalk, coming to rest as it embedded itself in the front doorway of a restaurant.

The collision allowed Kasey to close the gap as they crossed Lexington Avenue. Construction along East 56th Street further narrowed the roadway, bringing Kasey perilously close to the vehicles parked along the right-hand side of the street.

If any of them are foolish enough to pull out without looking, they are going to get annihilated.

Bishop pointed ahead. "Kasey, watch out."

Kasey squinted through the windshield and her heart skipped a beat—they were on a collision course with the police cordon. In an effort to contain the collateral damage, West had progressively tightened the cordon around Park Avenue. At the intersection of 56th and 3rd Avenue, the police had set up a roadblock. Squad cars lined the street, but in front of them was a solid wall of concrete bollards. Any attempt to ram the barrier was likely to result in flipping the vehicle.

Akihiro must have reached the same conclusion as he veered violently to the left, turning up 3rd Avenue. Kasey made to follow him but found the Bearcat's turning circle far wider than she had anticipated.

Reaching over, Bishop yanked down on the steering wheel. "You have to put your back into it, Kasey."

The police officers at the cordon watched in shock as the armored transport swung wide around the corner, missing them by mere feet. In spite of Bishop's added help, Kasey still slammed into the flank of a convertible, shunting the sports car onto the sidewalk. Its alarm blared as Kasey pulled back onto the street.

Up ahead, Akihiro was turning left, this time onto East 57th Street.

Kasey punched the gas. This time, she was ready. Starting wide, she yanked down on the wheel. The Bearcat swung around the corner, and she reversed her rotation of the wheel to bring the vehicle back into the lane seconds before the Bearcat would have obliterated a Toyota Prius.

"So, you slaughter the convertible and spare the Prius?" Bishop said. "West is going to be just thrilled when the department gets the bill for that, you know."

"If we live through today, they can be grateful they are replacing a car, not rebuilding the city from the ground up," Kasey replied as she took off after Akihiro.

For three blocks, she chased him back toward Park Avenue, blitzing past retail stores and office buildings. Akihiro stopped for no one and nothing. As he reached Park Avenue, he veered left to head down the city's uncharacteristically empty thoroughfare.

Kasey followed him around the corner, managing to keep her pedal flat to the floor. The heavy vehicle slid around, but the abandoned 5th Avenue was wide enough to accommodate the desperate maneuver. Kasey pushed the Bearcat to its limits, but Akihiro was clearly doing the same with his as it seemed impossible to close the distance between them. He powered down Park Avenue, the long straight allowing them to pick up speed.

Flashing lights indicated the police roadblock that had sealed the street ahead. Fifth Avenue was far wider than the smaller side streets, but the NYPD had nonetheless clogged both lanes with vehicles and concrete barriers.

Akihiro didn't slow, his Bearcat powering toward the barrier with reckless abandon.

"He's not gonna stop," Bishop shouted over the roaring engine.

Kasey gripped the wheel tighter until the knuckles on both her hands turned white. "Then neither are we. Hang on!"

Akihiro veered at the last minute, mounting the median strip and running straight through the roadblock at the point of least resistance.

Two police sedans overlapped the median strip. Akihiro collided with them, smashing through them as if they were nothing more than a wet paper bag. The two police sedans spiraled across the intersection with their steel hood panels dragging uselessly against the asphalt.

As the sedans came to a standstill, Kasey took aim at the same gap. She burst through the narrow chasm Akihiro had created, much to the bewildered surprise of the onlooking police officers.

As the pair of vehicles rolled down Park Avenue, Bishop spoke up. "Kasey, if that was the cordon, the streets ahead are going to get busier. We need to stop him before he reaches them or there is going to be serious collateral damage. That thing is a tank. If it plows through traffic like he just did that roadblock, he could kill dozens, maybe even hundreds of people. We need to stop him now."

"You need to take out his tires," Kasey said.

Bishop studied the rear of Akihiro's vehicle as it sped down 5th Avenue.

Shaking her head, she replied, "There's no way in hell I'll make that shot. It's an impossible angle."

"Well, we aren't going to catch him like this," Kasey answered through gritted teeth. "Take the wheel."

Bishop reached over and grabbed the Bearcat's steering wheel. With her hands free, Kasey rolled down the window and leaned out.

A bullet might not do it, but Kasey had other ideas. She focused on the rear wheels of the Bearcat in front of them.

Drawing deep, she channeled everything she had into one last spell. "*Ffrwydrad Aer.*"

Akihiro's vehicle swerved wildly as both rear wheels exploded simultaneously. With the tires punctured, the vehicle started losing speed.

Akihiro powered on regardless. The rear wheels sparked against the asphalt as the tires shredded.

Kasey leaned back inside the cab. "That ought to do it. Now we just have to bring him to a stop."

Kasey quickly reeled in the wounded Bearcat. As soon as she reached it, she began to overtake it on the right-hand side.

The Master of the Shinigami veered to the right to cut them off. The sudden maneuver shunted Kasey toward the edge of the street and onto the footpath. She wrenched the wheel down and to the left, pulling back onto the street, before stepping on the gas once more. As they caught up to him, Akihiro began to drift across the street, blocking their approach.

"This time don't try to overtake him," Bishop replied. "You just need to get up behind him on the right-hand side, nice and close. You want to put your left-hand side of the hood right up beside his right wheel."

Kasey followed Bishop's directions. Narrowing the gap, she started to ease off the gas, so that they sidled up beside Akihiro.

"Closer, closer," Bishop urged her on.

Kasey edged over inch by inch until the vehicles were practically touching.

"Okay, now yank left on the wheel, and when he spins out, just accelerate straight through him," Bishop said.

"He'll spin out?" Kasey asked.

"Sure will. Won't be able to do anything about it either. He won't have enough traction to do anything. He'll be right where we want him." Bishop replied

Yanking down on the wheel, Kasey veered left straight through Akihiro's rear wheel well. As she struck the back end of Akihiro's transport, it indeed slid out. Akihiro tried to correct but only served to throw the vehicle into a greater spin. The armored transport swerved wildly to the right, directly in front of Kasey's Bearcat.

Realizing Bishop's meaning, Kasey accelerated. The vehicle leapt forward, smashing into the right-hand flank of Akihiro's transport. Both vehicles slowed as Akihiro's carrier was shunted sideways up the street, driven onward by Kasey's vehicle wedged solidly in its flank. Easing to the right, Kasey steered both vehicles directly toward the wall of the People's United Bank.

"Brace yourself," Bishop shouted as the Bearcats burst onto the sidewalk and careened into the stone wall of the bank.

Kasey was thrown forward in her seat. If not for the seatbelt, she would have been obliterated by the windshield at almost forty miles an hour. The seatbelt caught her and tossed her back into the seat.

Kasey regathered her senses and scanned the wreckage in front of her. Akihiro's Bearcat was pinned between them and the wall, its buckled frame twisted by the impact with a steady plume of smoke rising from its hood.

She pushed open her door. Undoing her seatbelt, she fell more than climbed down from the cab. Hitting the sidewalk, she stumbled into the side of the Bearcat. She rested against the cool steel for a moment, as she caught her breath. Looking up at the ruined Bearcat, she saw Akihiro for the first time since the crash. His crumpled figure was jammed up against the glass.

Seeing her target so close filled Kasey with renewed strength. Taking a deep breath to calm her nerves, she crept toward the ruined vehicle.

Chapter 17

Kasey stalked through the debris to Akihiro's transport. Smoke poured from the ruined vehicle. Bracing herself, she climbed up the side of the cab and peered in the window. He lay awkwardly over the steering wheel and dash. Worried about a trap, she watched him for a moment. When he didn't stir, she wrenched open the door.

He groaned but didn't rise.

"If I'd been alive for centuries, I'd like to think I'd be wise enough to wear a seatbelt," Kasey chided.

He twitched. Leaning over, Kasey studied his injuries. Being hurled into the dash had likely caused internal bleeding. He was also sporting a series of nasty bruises including one across the right side of his face, probably where he had impacted the steering wheel.

Kasey rolled him over. As she did so, she discovered the skull shaped amulet around his neck shining brightly.

Swirling green smoke surrounded the amulet.

"If that's not the best case of karma I've ever seen," Kasey muttered. The Shinigami's own life force was being drained by the amulet.

Kasey leaned closer, her eyes fixated on the mesmerizing flow of energy. As she watched the emerald energy, she realized it wasn't flowing into the amulet, but from it.

The life force was pouring out of the skull and flowing straight into the Master of the Shinigami, the tendrils of emerald energy being absorbed into his wounded frame.

It's healing him, Kasey realized with a start. Every second that passed, he would be regaining strength.

Kasey grabbed him by his belt and dragged him toward her.

Akihiro stirred but before he could respond, Kasey yanked his necklace free and then shoved him from the cab. He plummeted to the sidewalk and slammed into the concrete. As he struck the ground, he doubled over with a groan.

Kasey clambered down from the cab. As she did, Akihiro reached out and placed his hands on the sidewalk. Slowly, he pushed himself to his feet.

"You have harassed me for long enough, Miss Chase," he said, grasping for his amulet. As his hands grasped nothing but air, he looked down, his eyes growing wide. "What?"

"Looking for this?" Kasey asked as she raised the amulet. The emerald energy swirled about her hand, and her entire arm tingled. "I can see why you like it. I feel better already. It's like the weight of the world has been lifted off my shoulders."

"You fool, you tamper with magic beyond your understanding," he said, narrowing his eyes at her. "That energy you're feeling is the legacy of a thousand lost souls whose spirits have been trapped in that device for eons. It took me years to learn how to harness its powers properly. It is realms beyond your abilities."

Kasey studied the amulet. She could feel the power pulsing from it. It was begging to be unleashed. Her arm twitched as the artifact's energy fought for release. The feeling of so much power at her fingertips was intoxicating. She could understand how Akihiro had grown so arrogant. The amulet made her feel invincible.

Such a sensation would be a seductive and dangerous lie.

Whoever had created the cursed artifact had likely become its first victim, no doubt feeling untouchable until the very moment it had failed them. Even now, Kasey longed to keep it.

After all, who would part with such a powerful trinket? a seductive voice whispered in her mind. *Think of all you could do. Think of all the lives you might save.*

Kasey tore her eyes away from the skull and looked at Akihiro. He was fixated on the amulet.

"It's potent," Kasey whispered. "I have to give it that. It's almost enough to make me want to keep it."

"Almost?" Akihiro straightened. "Never! Give it back and your death will be swift and painless. Deny me, and I will ensure your suffering endures until all you know, and love is dust."

"Always so full of yourself, Akihiro," Kasey chided. "Don't worry. I'll not be keeping it. There's only one thing to do with such a dangerous relic."

She drew on the power of the amulet, and it surged down her arm and into her being. She felt her body fill with arcane energy. It seemed like she was floating on a bed of limitless energy. Then, without warning, it soured. The same sickening sensation she had endured as Akihiro's magic had been manifested filled her to her core. Her face twisted in agony as the heart wrenching sorrow overwhelmed her.

Akihiro laughed. "I told you, you are too weak to possess the amulet."

Kasey fought the pain within.

Shaking her head, she replied, "I have no intention of possessing it."

She retreated from the pain and withdrew into the fortress of her inner mind. Focusing every facet of her will upon the amulet pulsing in her hand, she drew all she could from it, harnessing the energy into a shield for herself. Then, she channeled the balance of the energy back into the amulet with one intention: destroying the artifact.

"What are you doing?" Akihiro shouted.

Kasey couldn't answer, pain radiated through her being as the corrupted artifact resisted her intentions. Its magic burned within her causing Kasey's entire frame to shake uncontrollably. The amulet glowed brighter and brighter. She changed her grip to the chain as it began to overheat. The silver skull turned an angry red and began to melt. Emerald life force streamed from the artifact.

"No!" Akihiro shouted as the amulet dissolved. Sloughs of molten steel dripped onto the sidewalk as a shrill scream split the evening air.

For a moment, Kasey thought the scream was Akihiro, but it grew in intensity until the amulet exploded.

The blast slammed into Kasey's shield and sent her flying. She tucked her head and rolled as she hit the sidewalk. The impact paled compared to the pain she had felt as the amulet had been destroyed. Kasey went to rise but Akihiro was already looming over her.

In his hand, he held the same slender weapon he had used to kill John.

"You'll pay for that," he said with a snarl. "You will beg for an end to your suffering and it will not come."

Kasey's gaze was locked on the blade. Something about the glinting energy playing across its blade was entrancing. Now she realized why both John and Arthur had been unable to move. It was hauntingly beautiful.

The blade must also be magic.

Akihiro brought the blade down. Kasey willed her body to move, but she could not.

As its wicked point descended, a gunshot rang out.

Kasey looked up to see a blossom of red forming on Akihiro's robe. Two more gunshots rang out. Each time, the Master of the Shinigami bucked involuntarily as the bullets hit him.

His eyes went wide as every beat of his heart pumped his precious blood out of his body.

He dropped the blade.

As soon as it left his hand, the spell was broken. Kasey felt her limbs respond once more.

The blade plunged toward the sidewalk. Kasey reached out and snatched it by the hilt. Raising it, she lunged forward and drove it through Akihiro's chest. His mouth dropped open as the blade burst through his back.

Kasey pushed herself to her feet

Akihiro spat out a mouthful of blood. "How?"

Kasey slowly turned Akihiro until he was facing Bishop. She was standing on the ledge of the truck, battered but unbroken, her pistol raised, smoke wafting from its barrel

"Now, that shot, Chase. I can make that shot all day long."

Kasey smiled as she leaned in. "You see, Akihiro, I don't use and discard everyone who crosses my path. How does it feel to know you were bested by a normal?"

Akihiro grunted. Paralyzed by the blade, there was nothing he could do.

"I think not, Kasey." Akihiro panted. "This deed will be laid at your feet. The Brotherhood will seek recompense."

Kasey shoved him away from her. His mouth twisted into a grin as he slid free of the blade. Before he could react, Kasey brought it back across her body in one sweeping horizontal stroke.

Akihiro's head rolled off his shoulders and struck the sidewalk.

Kasey dropped the blade and sank. Reaching for the truck behind her, she found its tire and collapsed against it.

"It's over," Kasey whispered. "At last, it's over."

Bishop slid down beside her. "It sure is. You did it, Kasey. You beat them."

CHAPTER 18

Kasey pushed open the wooden door to the Administorum's recovery ward. The pristine room was one she was all too familiar with. She'd spent days holed up in a suite just like this. Curtains surrounded each of the room's occupants.

She wandered over to the first bed and swept aside the curtain. Lying on the bed was Noah Sanders.

Sanders eyes lit up. "Kasey, it's so good to see you. You're just the person I wanted to speak with."

"Oh, yeah?" Kasey replied, dropping into the chair by the bed. "That can't be good."

"Oh, I just wanted to lay eyes on the savior of New York City," Sanders replied as the edges of his mouth crept up into a grin.

Kasey blushed. "Oh, shut up, I get enough outside. I don't need it from you. Besides, we both know the truth—you're the one that stopped the device."

Sanders sat up and shuffled back against the headboard. "I don't know about that. There aren't many witnesses to back your claim, Miss Chase. You, on the other hand, it seems half the city saw you finish Akihiro as he tried to flee the scene. Like it or not, you're trending. Hashtag KickAssKasey."

Kasey shook her head. "That's just what I needed. I can't even get a coffee without the barista bringing it up. When the world has seen you kill someone, even in self-defense, it changes things, and I can't stop it. Now, every kid with a smart phone is following me around, looking for the next big hit."

"Oh," Sanders replied. "There's going to be a sequel? Who's it going to be?"

"You, if you don't cut it out," she said with a laugh. "Any more of that from you, and I'm going to smother you with your pillow."

Sanders held up both arms in feigned protest, "Okay, okay. I surrender. I've had my fun. So, what brings you here?"

"I just wanted to see how you are doing," Kasey said, leaning back in her chair. "And I wanted to thank you for having the courage to stop the device."

Sanders waved the praise away with his one good hand. "It's nothing you wouldn't have done. If I'd let you, it would be you laying here instead of me and I don't know that I would have been able to stop Akihiro. I have the feeling that everything is as it is supposed to be. It was your vision that got us here. Your vision that saved the city. I think it had to be you to stop him. So, I'm glad you did."

Kasey shuffled awkwardly in her seat. Praise wasn't something she was used to, so she decided to change the subject. "Do you want to know what Akihiro said with his last breath?"

Sanders' smile faded. "Not particularly, but let's have it."

"He said that the Brotherhood would kill me for the part I played in his death." Kasey bit her lip nervously. "With all this media coverage, they are going to know exactly who I am. If Akihiro was telling the truth, they'll come for me."

Sanders reached out with his remaining hand and placed it on Kasey's. "If he's telling the truth, Kasey—and that's a very big if—we don't even know if this Brotherhood exists. Akihiro was a compulsive liar who would do and say anything to save his own skin."

Kasey shook her head. "They are real. Arthur Ainsley was murdered because he went to his priest to confess his involvement with them. Unfortunately, Akihiro had taken the priest's place and killed Arthur to silence him. Whoever the Brotherhood is, they are dangerous. The Master of the Shinigami, the former Chancellor of the Arcane Council. It's a powerful circle to move in."

Sanders rubbed Kasey's hand gently. "Kasey, you have to stop. You have to stop worrying and waiting for the worst. You've spent your whole life fighting this attack and you did it. You beat it. It's over. Brotherhood or no Brotherhood, Akihiro is dead and the threat he posed is gone. I led the ADI for years, Kasey. Trust me when I say there will always be another threat, another criminal, another foe. There will always be someone seeking their own gain at other's expense. Let them come. In the meantime, you need to enjoy life and make the most of it. You can't live in perpetual fear."

"Easy for you to say," Kasey grumbled. "You can't see them coming."

"True, but what do you see now?" Sanders asked.

Kasey hesitated. "Nothing. I haven't had a vision since the attack."

"Exactly. So, relax. For once, time is on our side."

In her heart, Kasey knew Sanders was right. There was no shortage of criminals in the city—the cases she'd worked with Bishop told her that much was true—but she needed to start living.

If the Brotherhood comes, so be it. I'll cross that bridge when I come to it.

In the meantime, she had other plans. Her struggle against the Shinigami had awakened in her a need to study her roots. She longed to better understand the world of magic. She wanted to hone her skills and test her limits, and Sanders knew more about it than anyone she had ever met.

Sanders chimed in. "There was something I wanted to talk to you about. You see, Kasey, there is a vacancy on the Arcane Council. It appears the last head of the ADI was a dashing fugitive who lucked into a promotion. They made him Chancellor and now the ADI is in need of a new boss."

Kasey shook her head. "Nope. No way. Not on your life."

Sanders reached out. "You'll do great, come on."

Kasey held up her hands. "Hell no. It's too much. The bureaucracy, the endless meetings, it would drive me mad. Besides, I spent so long running from the ADI that the thought of joining them, it just doesn't feel right. It's not me. I'd love to help, but I can't do that."

There was a lilting laugh that carried through the ward. It seemed to be coming from the neighboring bed.

"I told you, Sanders, she's never going to take your desk job," a familiar voice said.

Kasey leaned over and ripped aside the curtain.

Her jaw dropped as she took in the occupant of the second bed. There, hidden beneath layers of bandages, was Hades.

"You don't look so happy to see me, Chase," he said, his tone light-hearted. "I thought you'd be thrilled."

Kasey shook off her surprise. "Don't get me wrong, it's good to see you, Hades, but I thought you were..."

"Dead? Pushing up daisies? Dearly departed?" Hades finished her sentence

"Yeah, I dunno about dearly, but the rest of them."

"Ouch. I see what you mean, Sanders. No mercy at all," he replied, looking at Noah.

Kasey shook her head.

"How did you survive?" she asked.

Hades smiled. "Sometimes you just get lucky. Zryx put three in my back. The vest took two of them, but the third got through, so when I went down, I played dead. When the surviving agents mopped up the traitors, they managed to get me out and stabilized before I bled out. I'm lucky to be alive."

"Ewww," Kasey teased. "Owing your life to the ADI, that has to be a bitter pill to swallow for the king of the underworld."

Hades recoiled as if stung. "Oh? If I recall correctly, I saved all of you just this morning. Those Night Crew chaps were trying to blow your poor station to hell. As far as I can see, we're completely even. Besides, if you aren't going to work for the ADI, you could always come join me. I'm in need of a new lieutenant. Some rambunctious young woman barbecued the last one."

"She had it coming," Kasey replied. "Thanks for the offer, but no deal. I may have had a dalliance with the dark side, but I prefer being on this side of the law."

Hades shrugged. "Well, you can't blame a man for trying."

Sanders cleared his throat. "Okay, Kasey, final offer. I'll create a new unit, the Arcane Alliance. Entirely independent of the ADI infrastructure, its mandate will be to hunt down extraordinary threats to our community. With the Council decimated, I'm sure there will be others who will want to prey on our perceived weakness. I would have you lead the charge in our defense."

Kasey nodded. "The Arcane Alliance, I like the sound of that. Extraordinary threats, you say? I'm imagining that the Brotherhood would fall inside those parameters?"

Sanders smiled. "You never quit, do you?"

Kasey slowly shook her head, "I don't know how."

Sanders laughed. "Deal."

She reached forward and clasped his right hand.

"You will have to resign from your work at the Ninth Precinct," he said. "You'll be far too busy to be doing both."

Kasey paused. "I don't suppose you'll break the news to Bishop?"

"Bishop?" Sanders raised his eyebrows. "Not on your life. She terrifies me."

"You big chicken." Kasey laughed as she sank back into the chair.

Everything was changing so quickly, but for the first time, she felt like she was choosing her own path, rather than having it thrust upon her. It felt good.

"Another good one bites the dust." Hades sighed, rearranging his pillow.

For the first time since she was twelve years old, Kasey looked to the future and saw promise.

The End

The attack on New York City almost cost her everything. The 9th Precinct has been decimated. The few surviving members of the Arcane Council are fighting to protect the world of magic. The supernatural has been thrust into the spotlight, and New York City is not a fan. Rogue wizards roam the streets, and criminals from across the country are flocking to help themselves to the spoils of a city in chaos. This mayhem would just be another Monday for Kasey...if it wasn't for the freshly exsanguinated corpse in SoHo. Dive into A Taste Of Death today. Click here (or scan the QR code below).

Or for the paperback version, click here (or scan the QR code below).

Have you heard about the Kase files?

I have a series of exclusive short stories set in Kasey's world. I share them with my newsletter subscribers. You can join here for free (or scan the QR code below).

THANK YOU FOR BEING HERE

I hope you enjoyed *Until My Dying Day* and the *Conjuring A Coroner Series* thus far. It's been an absolute blast for me to write, and I hope you've enjoyed it too. Do not fear, while this is the end of this arc of Kasey's adventure, there is plenty more trouble brewing for her in New York City. If you read on, you'll find a preview for *A Taste of Death.* I also have several other series set in this universe. So you're in no danger of running out!

Before you roll on to the next book, I wanted to take a moment to thank you for being here! You've helped make this series a success and I appreciate it.

As a self-published author, I don't have the huge marketing machine of a traditional publisher behind me. In fact, it's just me, my laptop and a hunger to share my stories with the world.

Fortunately I have some of the best readers in the world. Every time you send a message or email, tell a friend about my series or share it on social media it helps me bring these worlds to life.

If you have enjoyed this book, I would love it if you could spend a minute or two to leave a rating or review for me (it can be as short or as long as you like), this link will take you to the right page.

Thank you, your support makes all the difference!

Until next time!

S. C. Stokes

P.S. I know many readers are hesitant to reach out to an author, fearing that they might get ignored. I am a reader at heart and know how you feel. I respond to every Facebook message and every email I receive.
You can find me on:

Facebook
Bookbub
Email: samuel@samuelcstokes.com

You can also visit my website where you can join my newsletter to enjoy some exclusive short stories and other Kasey related goodness.

A Taste With Death Preview

I t wasn't Kasey's first visit to the Training Pits but they never failed to impress. Big enough for three basketball courts side-by-side, the Training Pits adjoined the ADI's headquarters. This deep beneath the city, both magic and technology had played a part in their creation. Here in the relative safety of the Pits, the Battle Mages of the ADI practiced for combat.

The training pits had the look of a medieval gymnasium, and probably hadn't been refurbished in the past two decades. Overhead, ventilations fans whirred but failed dismally to remove the chamber's damp smell.

The equipment was well used and appeared well past its prime. Adjoining the Training Pits was a firing range and beside it stood a number of mannequins lined up neatly along the wall.

Kasey knew from her previous visit that they were far more durable than they appeared. Each of the worn figures had been enchanted to withstand an absolute pounding. Kasey had hit them with everything she had, from a cascading rain of fire, to a direct hit from a bolt of lightning. The dummies hadn't even been scratched. Not one to give up, Kasey had endeavored to sear through it with a pure beam of arcane energy, but it had reflected off the dummy with nothing but a slight singe mark to show for her effort. The sad reality was that after the training session, the only one that was any worse for wear was Kasey.

Today, the Pits were empty, Sanders having reserved them for their weekly dueling lessons.

Kasey hung her coat by the door, set her case file on the counter and wandered over to Sanders, "So, Obi-Wan, what do you have in store for me today?"

Sanders stood by a wooden table and was lifting lead cylinders out of a crate onto the counter with his good hand. Each cylinder was the size of a milk carton and weighed several pounds. Sanders proceeded to stack ten of the cylinders into a pyramid, much like a side show alley game.

"Before we get into that," he said, "tell me how your readiness exercises are going from last week?"

"Pretty well, I think. I used them this morning actually. I didn't end up needing my magic, but if I did, I'd have been ready. I'm definitely seeing their value."

"What happened this morning?" Sanders asked, his hands resting on his hips.

The question had a bit of an edge on it. He was not the relaxed Noah she was used to dealing with in their private sessions. With the newly announced Laws of Magic, she was a little reluctant to tell him what had happened.

"Who is asking? My friend Noah, or the Arcane Chancellor?"

Sanders smiled. "Your friend, of course."

Kasey met his smile with one of her own. "Just checking. Bishop had me swing by a crime scene. Wanted my opinion on a body they found. She thought it might have a supernatural perp, but I doubt it."

"Didn't get a vision off the body?" Sanders asked.

"Nope. Still radio silence on that front," Kasey replied. "But we had a promising run-in with some local enforcers. I thought things might get hairy, but it turned out all right in the end. As far as I can tell, it was simply a disagreement between rival loan sharks. One of the customers wound up dead and Bishop is going to run it down."

Sanders fiddled with the glove on his left hand. "Sorry to task you up with a case in there, but it's an important one, Kasey. After what Akihiro did to the city, the community is still on edge. We need to do everything we can to try and bring our people together. Outside our own community, everyone's a little afraid of us. People are paranoid that the next maniacal wizard might just succeed. We need them to know we are here to protect them. If it turns out a wizard did light that fire..." Sanders paused, unable to finish the thought.

Kasey ran her hand through her hair. "I'll take a look. I'm not sure how much good it will do. Most of my expertise is with bodies, not burnt-out buildings."

Sanders cocked his head. "Don't sell yourself short. You're probably our world's leading authority on torching buildings in Manhattan."

She gave him a playful shove.

"But seriously, whatever you can do would be appreciated," Sanders said. "The ADI can't touch this one, but we still need answers."

"It's going to tie-up some time though. Hard to chase down the Brotherhood while I'm sifting through ashes in Brooklyn."

"Well," Sanders began. "You could always hire some help like I've been telling you."

Kasey scrunched up her face a little. "I don't know. What if someone got injured following my lead? It's one thing when you're taking all the risks yourself, another when it's someone else's life at stake."

Her gaze hovered down to the glove on Sander's left wrist. She had hesitated, and Sanders had given his hand, literally, to defuse the device that would have destroyed Manhattan.

Sanders caught her stare.

"It's not your fault, Kasey. I've told you before, and I'll tell you again. It was my choice to defuse the device. I knew the price when I made the call. You didn't make me do it."

"I didn't stop you either," she replied. "Everyone thinks I'm a hero. No one knows that it's really you they have to thank."

"It was a team effort. I got the bomb. You got Akihiro. Don't worry about the kudos. Its better this way. You distract the media for a few news cycles and while everyone's busy, we'll try to set a narrative that won't result in the world trying to burn us at the stake this time," he replied.

Kasey leaned against the table and pushed her hair back behind her ear. She knew what Sanders was saying was true, but it didn't make her feel any better about it.

"Once things quiet down, I'll have the time to finish working on a replacement for this," he said, tapping the prosthesis. "I have some ideas, but they aren't ready for a field test yet. When it is, you'll be the first to see it."

Kasey smiled. There was ring of hope in his voice. The combination of the stress of his new position and the loss of his hand had really been getting him down lately.

Happy looked good on him. She wished she saw a little more of it.

"So, what are these for?" Kasey asked, pointing at the stacked cylinders.

"Today, we're working on something a little different. I can't tell you, otherwise it will defeat the point of the lesson."

"Ok. Cryptic. I'll bite. What do you want me to do?"

Sanders grinned. "I want you to take ten steps back, then I want you to knock them over. More importantly, I want you to get all of them, in a single strike."

"That's what I'm talking about," Kasey muttered.

The last few lessons had been useful, but had been a little passive for her tastes. Sanders was a master; she wanted to learn some of the devastating spells she had seen him employ.

She took the ten steps and turned to face the table. "You might want to take a few steps back."

"Fair enough." Sanders chuckled as he went to stand by the dummies.

Closing her eyes, Kasey felt for the arcane energy about her. She pictured scattering the cylinders like a prize pitcher might at the knock'em downs.

Opening her eyes, she said, "*Dwrnyrawyr.*"

A rush of wind hurtled forth from her outstretched hand, buffeting the table. The weighted cylinders didn't move an inch.

"They're heavier than they appear," Sanders replied. "Try again."

Kasey summoned her will and bellowed, "*Mellt.*"

Lightning arced from her hand at the stack of cylinders. The impact knocked two cans loose, before the lightning ground itself.

Sanders muttered a spell and mist played over the cylinders, like a fire extinguisher. He scooped up the toppled cylinders and put them back into place.

Those had been two of her favorite combat spells, and they had barely made a dint.

Kasey considered summoning an inferno to reduce the annoying cylinders to a pile of molten slag. It wouldn't be quick, but it would have the desired effect. The table would certainly give out first though.

Kasey smiled to herself as she saw the loophole.

Ignoring the cylinders entirely, she focused her energy on the wooden table beneath them. She pictured the grain running through the timber.

"*Hollt!*" she said.

The spell hit the timber. There was an earsplitting crash as the table gave out, the lead cylinders clattering to the ground, sending weights and debris in every direction.

Sanders clapped. "Now you're thinking!"

Kasey grinned, dusting her hands together.

Sanders approached her. "I have watched you in action. As an elementalist, you have a natural affinity for destructive magic. You are a more than capable practitioner in spite of the sparseness of your training. The problem with natural talent is that one day you are going to come across someone who is simply more powerful than you. They'll be more knowledgeable, or simply have stronger enchantments at their disposal. They will outlast you, and could well kill you. Not every battle is won through raw power. In fact, when dueling, more battles will be decided in your mind, before they are won on the battlefield. It is the duelist with the swiftest mind that triumphs."

Kasey smoothed her palms against her jeans. She had faced that dilemma in the battle with Akihiro. Try as she might, he'd simply had too much power. He had spent his life stealing the life force from others and binding it in his amulet. There had been no hope for her to outlast him. He had bat her aside like a child. She'd watched him wade through a firefight, bring down a helicopter, and unleash torrents of destructive energy and still he had more than enough power left. It wasn't until she'd destroyed the amulet that she had leveled the playing field. Of course, the bullets Bishop had put in him had helped too.

"Today's lesson is all about the subtle art of making a little magic go a long way. This way, if you are caught against superior numbers, you won't burn out trying to push through them all. I'll teach you to disable and deter while retaining your reserves of power, rather than rampaging through your enemies like a derailed freight train, hoping you have enough juice in the tank to make it through."

Kasey levelled an accusatory finger at Sanders. "I take your point, but you have to remember, I have seen you in action and you do one of the finest impressions of a freight train I've ever seen."

She was referring to Sander's favorite spell, one that seemed to combine a blinding corona of light with an explosive charge. The resulting power was unlike anything she'd ever seen and the

Chancellor had used it to devastating effect. She'd seen him at work in the Ainsley's Manor and again as they had fled the Night Crew stash house. The power involved had to be considerable. Sanders almost looked like a mini sun going supernova, blinding to look at and while not as destructive as the cosmic event, those caught in its radius would be too dead to know the difference.

"Every dog has their day," Sanders replied. "You'll note each time I expend that much power, it was at the conclusion of the engagement. A final gambit to level the playing field or end the conflict. Opening with such moves is foolish and leaves you exposed to your enemy's attacks. Every wizard has their limit, Kasey. If you push your body too hard, the magic you're channeling will tear you apart."

"I know, I know," Kasey replied. Pushing herself was almost second nature. It was a fate she had to be more wary of. "Still, one day you're going to have to teach me how you do it."

"We will see," Sanders said. "Baby steps."

"What's next?" she asked, surveying the destruction she had wrought on the table.

Sanders looked at her. "Now we try the principle in action. Give me everything you've got. I'm going to show you how you can protect yourself without having to rely entirely on wards and shields."

"What's wrong with wards and shields?" Kasey asked.

"Nothing is wrong with them, per se," Sanders said, "but they bog you down and commit you to a course of action that isn't always in your best interest. The more punishment your shield takes, the more energy it drains from you. If you commit to one against a more powerful opponent, they will simply wear you down. They don't even have to be more powerful than you—they could simply be more numerous. Learning how to protect yourself without resorting to these, will give you greater flexibility and make you more dangerous in the field."

"More dangerous." Kasey flexed in jest. "I like the sound of that."

Sanders walked across the chamber until he stood at the other end of the room.

"Give me everything you've got," he called. "Don't hold back."

It was a trap, but she wasn't going to give Sanders the satisfaction of her backing down from the challenge. Watching Sanders in action was the best education she could get. She just didn't want to embarrass herself in front of him.

Raising both hands, Kasey chanted, "*Pêl Tân.*"

A ball of flames coalesced above each of her outstretched hands and with a thought, Kasey hurled them both at Sanders, one after the other. He raised his good hand, his lips moving. Kasey couldn't catch the words over the furor of the flames crackling toward Sanders. A wind rippled through the chamber. Wind met fire and dispersed it effortlessly. Embers spiraled back toward her, carried on the breeze.

Not to be outdone she said, "*Mellt.*"

As the power cackled around her wrist, Sanders was already raising his hands. The lead cylinders along with the broken table twitched, rising into the air as Kasey let loose the bolt of lightning. Her spell slammed into the levitating cans arcing between them, before Sanders allowed them to fall back to the floor in a heap.

"Is that all you've got?" he taunted. "Come on, you can do better than that."

Kasey's mind raced. Sanders was trying to prove a point, but her pride wouldn't allow her to give up this easily. If she wanted to force Sanders' hand, she was going to need to go bigger.

Drawing in a deep breath, she formed a circle in her mind around the Chancellor. As she exhaled, she whispered, "*Tân.*"

Flames erupted along the line Kasey had imagined, a semicircle of fire meant to hem Sanders in, cutting down his options. With a thought, the flames grew. If Sanders tried wind again, it would be just as liable to feed the inferno.

Sanders attempted it anyway. The wall of fire flickered, almost changing course, but Kasey pushed her mind and will into the flames, feeding more power into the inferno. Sanders raised his black leather gloved prosthesis but nothing happened.

Kasey bit her lip.

That can't be right.

Sanders wasn't one to waste effort. Was he trying to distract her?

She tried to maintain her assault but out of her periphery, she spotted movement. Tearing her eyes off Sanders, she realized three of the practice dummies had sprang to life, and were charging across the chamber at her.

"Cheater," Kasey groaned in frustration.

Animation wasn't something she'd covered in her training.

She'd thought she'd had Sanders on a timer, but with a motion he'd turned the tables on her.

Sweat ran down her brow. Kasey looked across the chamber. The flames were growing, almost completely obscuring Sanders. Before he disappeared behind the flames, he raised his glove to his mouth as if yawning.

"Ass," Kasey muttered.

The first of the dummies crash-tackled Kasey to the ground. Kasey rolled, throwing the dummy free. Her spell dissipated, but Kasey had too much on her plate to deal with it. She swept her leg, tripping the second dummy, sending it crashing to the stone floor. The third piled on top of her, pinning her down.

To Be Continued.

Join Kasey on her latest case in A Taste of Death. Click here (or scan the QR code below).

ABOUT THE AUTHOR

Sam is a writer of magically-charged fantasy adventures. His passion for action, magic and intrigue spawned his Arcanoverse—a delightfully deluded universe that blends magic, myth, and the modern world in a melting pot that frequently explodes.

When he isn't hiding away in his writing cave, his favorite hobbies include cooking, indulging sugary cravings, gaming, and trying to make his children laugh. You can find more of his work at www.samuelcstokes.com or connect with him at the links below.

Also By S.C. Stokes

Conjuring A Coroner Series

A Date With Death

Dying To Meet You

Life Is For The Living

When Death Knocks

One Foot In The Grave

One Last Breath

Until My Dying Day

A Taste Of Death

A Brush With Death

A Dance With Death

Death Warmed Up

Death Sentence

Magical Midlife Crisis Series

Bounty Hunter Down Under

A Bay Of Angry Fae

Ghosts At The Coast

Urban Arcanology Series

Half-Blood's Hex

Half-Blood's Bargain

Half-Blood's Debt

Half-Blood's Birthright

Half-Blood's Quest

A Kingdom Divided Series

A Coronation Of Kings

When The Gods War

A Kingdom In Chaos

Bones Of The Fallen

A Siege Of Lost Souls